■ ▫ ■ ▫ ■

CONVERSATION WITH SPINOZA

D1552652

Writings from an Unbound Europe

■ □ ■ □ ■

GOCE SMILEVSKI

CONVERSATION WITH SPINOZA

A COBWEB NOVEL

Translated from the Macedonian by Filip Korženski

NORTHWESTERN UNIVERSITY PRESS

EVANSTON, ILLINOIS

Northwestern University Press
www.nupress.northwestern.edu

Copyright © 2006 by Northwestern University Press. Published 2006. All rights reserved.

Printed in the United States of America

10 9 8 7 6 5 4 3 2 1

ISBN 0-8101-2375-4 (cloth)
ISBN 0-8101-2376-2 (paper)

Library of Congress Cataloging-in-Publication Data

Smilevski, Goce.
  [Razgovor so Spinoza. English]
  Conversation with Spinoza : a cobweb novel / Goce Smilevski ; translated from the Macedonian by Filip Korženski.
    p. cm. — (Writings from an unbound Europe)
  ISBN 0-8101-2375-4 (cloth : alk. paper) — ISBN 0-8101-2376-2 (pbk. : alk. paper)
  1. Spinoza, Benedictus de, 1632–1677—Fiction. 2. Philosophers—Netherlands—Fiction. 3. Netherlands—Intellectual life—17th century—Fiction. I. Korženski, Filip. II. Title. III. Series
  PG1196.29.M58R3913   2005
  891.81936—dc22

2005036780

■ □ ■ □ ■

CONTENTS

■ □ ■ □ ■

CONVERSATION WITH SPINOZA

■ □ ■ □ ■

A NOTE TO THE READER

The threads of this novel are spun out of conversations between you and Spinoza. So wherever there is an empty space in the words of Spinoza, just say your name and write it in the blank space.

■ □ ■ □ ■

THREAD ONE

Encounter

You are lying dead on your bed and I am slowly approaching you. You look incredibly small, Spinoza, lying on this large red-velvet bed, on this canopied four-poster bed where you were born forty-four years and three months before your death. You are lying on this large red-canopied bed, the only possession you had. Now you no longer possess even the body that is lying on this bed, the body that you perhaps did not even possess while you were alive, while you still inhabited it.

I am looking at your dead body, from this distance, hundreds of years after your death, a moment before anyone has entered the room, before anyone has found your cold body. I am touching your hand: it is still warm. While I am touching it briefly, I can feel how the cold spreading all over your body is engulfing me too. A tear is drying on your cheek, and the people who will find you lying dead in your room will not be able to see it. They will find you lying curled up like a fetus, with your hair not properly combed and your mouth slightly open, as though it wished to say something or start a conversation. Your skin is translucent like Chinese paper and your nails unusually thick and dark yellow. But no one will notice the trace of the tear on your cheek—the tear will have dried up.

Why am I standing here, Spinoza, beside your dead body? Why am I standing so close to you, only a step away from your dead body, and yet so far away—hundreds of years after your death? Is it perhaps because of that tear, Spinoza, which has continued to exist as the essence of your life even after your life came to an end?

■ □ ■ □ ■

There is no tear on my face, _____. You are fairly close to me, _____, only a step away from my body, and yet very far from me—hundreds of years after my death. Like in an optical illusion where, owing to the bending of the light, the eye perceives some things in a different way from what they really are in space; in this case, owing to the bending of time, you see a tear that is not there—yes, you stand here, beside my body, but it is hundreds of years after my death. Besides, people who have read my books know very well how much I despised tears. To understand my contempt for tears, however, one should look at my whole life, not just the hour of my death. So I would suggest that you begin with my birth or, even better, the moment when I was conceived.

One February Night in Amsterdam

It is the end of February, it is nighttime, and Amsterdam is asleep. Merchants and priests are asleep, rich and poor alike are asleep, robbers and the robbed are asleep, as are those in love, loved ones, and abandoned ones; children and old people are asleep too, milkmen and masons are also asleep, the good and the bad people of Amsterdam are asleep as well, and although it is flowing, even the water in the canals is asleep. The whole of Amsterdam is asleep, and yet there are some people who are not sleeping this February night. The drunks are awake singing in the taverns between Jodenbreestraat and the Old Church; the harlots are awake and are walking the streets, stopping in front of the taverns and shouting their prices: some are pulling strangers by the sleeve, and others have already given their bodies to a sailor or a London merchant in the street. A man lying in prison who killed his wife and her young lover, having caught them in bed together, is also awake: tomorrow he is to be executed. A girl playing the harpsichord is awake as well, as is a young man reading *The Anatomy of Melancholy* by Robert Burton. An old woman who is to die this night is also sleepless, trying to remember the first night of her marriage. A fisherman is awake thinking of his hungry children; his children are awake as well because of their hunger, but, aware of his concerns, they pretend to sleep. A painter is not sleeping this night either: only a few houses away from the home in which you are to be born, he is standing with his sketches scattered around the room, preparing to paint a canvas. His name is Rembrandt. Your parents, Spinoza, are also awake, only a hundred meters away from the painter who is standing with anticipation in front of his canvas. They are lying in the darkness on the large red-canopied bed. Rembrandt is standing before his easel: he is looking at the drawing he has made with chalk on the canvas. The canvas shows a dead man—his name is Aris Kindt and he was executed on 16 January for armed robbery. A day after his execution, the president of the Guild of Surgeons, Nicolaes Tulp, and six of his colleagues invited Rembrandt to paint them during their anatomy lesson in the Anatomy Theater (*Theatrum Anatomicum*). Now, a month later, Rembrandt is still standing in front of his canvas, intent on finally beginning to paint the scene. He is standing close to the white surface with his brush soaked in red paint, just as your parents are lying close to each other this night. The empty space between their bodies is shortly to disappear. "Where should I begin?" asks Rembrandt, although his brush is soaked in bloodred paint. He looks at his sketches: the insides of the dead man's arm have been exposed through the use of forceps keeping the flesh in place. Nicolaes Tulp is the man holding the forceps: seven surgeons have gathered around the dead man's body—one of them, in the farthest left-hand section of the painting, is watching Tulp closely, apparently eager to hear what the professor has to say. The two people in the background are looking at the artist—their goal is obviously to be portrayed as splendidly as possible in the painting. One of them is focusing somewhere beyond the painting, possibly on the crowd of Amsterdam citizens who have gathered to see the sketching of the group portrait with the dead man. The man stooping over the most looks at the flesh exposed by the forceps. Two people are looking at the fingers of Professor Tulp's left hand—between his thumb and index finger he has a drop of blood. "Should I begin from this drop?" Rembrandt asks himself this night (this same night when you are about to be conceived, Spinoza). Hesitant, time after time he draws the brush close to the canvas, only to move it away a moment later: with similar short movements, although more quickly and without hesitation, the bodies of your parents are united. The expressions on their faces are reminiscent of the expression on Rembrandt's face. "How should I begin? Where should I begin?" are the questions the young painter repeats to himself. He is twenty-six and an accomplished painter, but demonstrates particular fear when he either has to begin or complete a painting. It is precisely at this moment that your parents are completing your conception: the semen of your father is injected into your mother's womb. "No," says Rembrandt to himself, "I'm not going to begin with the drop of blood. It is the essence of the soul, I'll leave it to the end," and he moves his brush, drawing the first red lines of the lifeless gaping flesh.

Eight Days after 24 November 1632

The name of the man who came to the Beth Jacob synagogue that morning carrying his son—born eight days earlier—was Michael Spinoza. Michael himself was born forty-five years earlier as Miguel Despinosa in Vidigere, Portugal, where his father, Isaac, had settled, moving from Lisbon and hoping that in the small town he would be able to observe the law of Moses with no fear of the Inquisition. He came into this world in 1587, exactly forty years after the establishment of the Inquisition Tribunal in the kingdom, whose principal goals were the forceful conversion of Jews and the prevention of converted Jews from going back to their original faith. He remembered a single event from his childhood: one hot summer night when he was nine he dreamed of huge fish flying in the sky with blood dripping from their mouths. It was then, in this dream, that he heard the voice of his mother, Mor Alvares, crying out to him from this side of reality. When he opened his eyes, he saw his mother and father hastily grabbing a few essentials: two loaves of bread, three handfuls of salt, a knife, a few tablespoons, a needle and yarn, and some clothing. While he was stepping over the threshold of his home for the last time together with his mother and brother and sister, he saw how his father Isaac kneeled in the room, pulled a plank up from the floor, took several books out, and put them under his arm. Later, when recollecting their flight, he would often take out one of those books, the Torah, and read Exodus again and again. At these times, he remembered again and again the tearful eyes of Mor Alvares staring at their little house, which grew ever smaller and smaller, vanishing into the distance, while no one traveling in the wagon drawn by two horses had any idea of where they were going. For a long time, from every town in which they found shelter, Mor Alvares would send a letter, which she had previously dictated to Isaac, to her brothers, not knowing whether her brothers were aware that their sister and her family had been indicted by the Inquisition for professing the Jewish religion. The Alvares family always sent their letters on the day they set off for another town, in case they were caught by the Inquisitors: the letters contained only the name of the town they had just left, the name of a place in that town, a date, and a signal. Mor Alvares believed that her brothers would understand her messages. If the letter said, "Ponte de Lima, marketplace near the courthouse, 14 August, picking your right nostril with the little finger of your left hand," it meant that she expected her brothers to appear on 14 August on the square near the courthouse in the town of Ponte de Lima, looking for a man who picked his right nostril with the little finger of his left hand, and that they were to give the same signal. In each of the towns in which they stayed for a few months, Mor Alvares and Isaac found a discreet Jew to whom they revealed the secret sign and the date on which he was supposed to appear in a particular place. They also mentioned to him the name of the town to which they were going so that the brothers would be able to find their sister. In all of the towns they passed through, Isaac and Mor Alvares left people jumping on one leg in the square, crouching and standing up near the harbor, or clapping their hands in front of the cathedral, but Mor Alvares's brothers never appeared. She often dreamed of a large piece of paper and the hands of her brothers writing something, but as she was illiterate, it was difficult for her to recognize the unfamiliar symbols and also to remember them so that her husband could interpret them all after she woke up. So she decided to learn how to read and write to be able to interpret her dreams. In every town they stayed in she learned three letters, and when she learned all the letters of the alphabet, she managed to read the following text in her dream: *To every thing there is a season, and a time to every purpose under the heaven: a time to be born, and a time to die; a time to plant, and a time to pluck up that which is planted; a time to kill, and a time to heal; a time to break down, and a time to build up; a time to weep, and a time to laugh; a time to mourn, and a time to dance; a time to cast away stones, and a time to gather stones together; a time to embrace, and a time to refrain from embracing; a time to get, and a time to lose; a time to keep, and a time to cast away; a time to rend, and a time to sew; a time to keep silence, and a time to speak;*

a time to love, and a time to hate; a time of war, and a time of peace." When she woke up, Mor Alvares spoke of her dream to her husband, but since she had already forgotten much of it, what she remembered was as scrappy as a dead body devoured by vultures: *"To every thing there is a season: a time to die; a time to pluck up that which is planted; a time to kill; a time to break down; a time to weep; a time to mourn; a time to cast away stones; a time to refrain from embracing; a time to lose; a time to cast away; a time to rend; a time to keep silence; a time to hate; a time of war."* The words sounded familiar to Isaac, but he could not remember where he had heard or read them. From that day on Mor Alvares had no more dreams and sent no more letters. She only hoped that one day she would find a comfortable home for all of them: for her children, Fernando, Miguel, Maria Clara; for her husband, Isaac; and for herself. The reply to all her letters arrived a month after she died in Nantes, France, in 1616. The reply came in the form of Sara, her brother Gabriel's daughter. While Sara was explaining that her father and the other two Alvares brothers had died, having been tortured at the hands of the Inquisitors, Miguel Despinosa, recently renamed Michel D'Espinoza, stared at the missing fingers of his cousin's left hand. Noticing his bewilderment, Sara put her fingerless hand close to his face and said: "They cut them off so that I cannot turn the pages of the Talmud they found under my pillow." A few days later, while sailing away from Nantes, leaving it for good, Michel D'Espinoza continued to gaze into the harbor until Sara's fingerless hand waving him good-bye disappeared into the distance. In Rotterdam he received his third name, Michael Spinoza, which he bore until his death. It was in this city that he had a premonition that the Dutch Republic would remain his home until his stay on earth came to an end. One day in November 1622, he moved to Amsterdam and married Rachel, the daughter of his uncle, Abraham. Toward the end of the following year, their first child died before it could even have been named on the eighth day after its birth, and in the autumn of 1624, their second child died at birth. Rachel fell gravely ill and became weaker and weaker. Soon, while sitting in front of her front door, she would have to put stones in her pockets so that the wind would not blow her away. She died one morning in February 1627, and the people who bathed her body said it was lighter than a seagull's wing. As soon as he arrived in Amsterdam, Michael had become active in commerce with the support of his uncle,

Abraham Spinoza. A year after the death of Rachel, Michael Spinoza married Hanna Deborah Senior, the daughter of Baruch Senior and Maria Nunes. Their daughter, Miriam, was born in 1629. A year later, Maria gave birth to their son, Isaac, and on 24 November 1632, they had another son.

The man who came to the Beth Jacob synagogue that morning in December 1632 was Michael Spinoza, and the eight-day-old child he brought to the shrine to be circumcised and given a name was me. The name they entered in the synagogue register was Bento Spinoza; they called me that at home and it was with that name that I became a merchant. I was registered as Baruch in the Talmud Torah school, and it was this name they used in the *cherem* through which my excommunication from the Jewish community was proclaimed. Following the *cherem,* the people called me Benedictus. All three names had the same meaning—"the blessed one"—the first in Portuguese, the second in Hebrew, and the third in Latin.

The world of my childhood began with a square. It was through that square—the window in one of the attic rooms of our home— that the world commenced: through the carob branches I was able to see the Houtgracht Canal that ran alongside the street in which we lived. Slightly to the left of our home was a bridge over the Houtgracht, linking the two sides of Vlooienburg. The view from the window of our attic extended to several houses on the other side of the canal: one of them was Beth Jacob, the synagogue where I was circumcised and where a name was given to me on the eighth day after my birth, and close to the synagogue were two houses that the Jewish community rented for the Talmud Torah school. We had rented the house we lived in from Willem Kiek, a silk dealer, and many people wondered why Michael Spinoza, who was not a particularly well-off merchant, had decided to reside on the Houtgracht itself and not in one of the backstreets of the interior of the island of Vlooienburg, where the poorer Jews lived.

The house we lived in had four rooms: on the ground floor there was a room where we ate, as well as a room we occupied during the day in the middle of which stood the large red-canopied bed. There were two rooms in the attic: in one of them my father kept some of the wines he sold in his shop, and we, the children, slept in the other room. It was through the window of that room that my childhood began, and the view from that room encompassed a piece of the sky, a street, a row of carob trees, a canal, a bridge across the canal, as well as several houses on the other side of the canal, including the synagogue and the school.

Religious instruction, which, as far as Jewish children were concerned, started in the home, continued in the houses across the canal—first in the synagogue (I remember my first visit there: while the young rabbi Aboab da Fonseca played the harp, the choir sang a hymn about the groom Israel and his bride Sabbath) and later in the school. I remember my father's face on the day he brought me to the synagogue for the first time and on my first day at school: his wish was that I become a rabbi.

We spoke Portuguese at home. We also spoke Spanish, since it was the language of literature, and Hebrew, as it was the language of the holy books. I later learned Dutch, although not well enough to use it in my writing.

My brother Gabriel was born when I was six. Giving birth to him, my mother, whom Father had often described as a sickly woman, fell seriously ill and within just five months, on 5 November 1638, died. Since then I have acquired the habit of sitting near the window through which the world began.

Continuance

I can imagine you sitting beside the window and looking outside. Didn't you wish that those moments before the death of your mother had turned into eternity? Didn't you wish, while gazing into the canal in front of your house and into the houses opposite, or above them into the sky, that every minute of the existence of your mother be transformed into endless continuance?

■ □ ■ □ ■

Mankind suffers from a seemingly harmless disease. The symptoms of this disease are made manifest through the superimposition of the characteristics of eternity and infinity to transient and finite things or events, and through the yearning that transient and finite things or events last forever. An old woman carries her grandson in her arms as they are walking over one of the bridges across the canals in

Amsterdam. Holding the child in her right arm, the old woman places a few coins in the palm of a florist standing on the bridge, and the florist hands a bunch of violets to the child. The child looks at the blue flowers and at that precise moment everything else disappears from the child's world: his grandmother, the florist's hand, the bridge and the canal water, the dark clouds, and the roofs of the houses—there is nothing else except the color of a few flowers in his hand—and a part of him (that part that is capable of believing) believes that this moment, this glimpse of those blue flowers will last forever, that his eyes will forever remain fixed on the violets, and that the blueness of the violets extends to the edge of space; the old woman who holds him in her arms knows that this vision will last for just a brief moment; she only yearns for such a moment to last forever and for the color of violets to expand infinitely. Both grandmother and grandson come to the New Church, and then continue along the street, passing the houses with the yellow façades. Close to one of the houses, which has a red door and whose doorstep is occupied by a sleeping cat, the child drops the flowers, while his grandmother continues to hold him in her arms and walk down the street. The flowers fall on the cat's head; it wakes up and scratches the red door with its claws; behind the door a child whose childhood has just ended lies on the bed covered with a sheet and masturbates for the first time in his life; at the moment he ejaculates he thinks that his pleasure will last forever, just as he believes that the images in his head that have aroused him to the point of masturbation will last. In the neighboring house, a left-handed boy leafs through using his right hand, the pages of *The Differences Between the Male and Female Body* by Andreas Vesalius and looks at the illustrations, while stimulating his penis with his left hand. He is aware that the pleasure will end, that he will have to wash his hands carefully, clean up the fluid on the floor, close the book, and go to school. While he puts his clothes on to go to school, he thinks of how wonderful it would be if, instead of listening to his teacher's instructions about the death of Jesus on the cross and the resurrection, he were able to masturbate eternally, and if the picture of the naked woman from *The Differences Between the Male and Female Body*, who plays with her braids with one hand and keeps the other hand on her hip, extended to infinity, taking up the space of his home, the street leading to his school, the school itself, and then extended even farther, across the whole of Amsterdam, if her breasts and hips stretched as far as Calvary, and even farther to the stars and beyond. Later, as he goes to school, the boy passes in front of a house where a man lies sick. The man suffers not so much from the pain of the illness itself, but more from the fear that the pain may last forever. There is, however, another thing that scares him even more than eternal pain: it is the belief that death, which will come at the end of his illness, will last forever. Death is not merely an instant for him.

This disease, let me repeat, may seem quite harmless, but is in fact fatal. Or rather, it is the only fatal disease. All other diseases kill what is mortal in man; this disease kills the immortal in him. Other diseases destroy the human body; this disease eliminates the possibility for any man to know the eternal and infinite and thus become a part of eternity and infinity. Anything less than eternity is not worth spending our time on; anything less than infinity is unworthy of exploration using our physical faculties. The only thing that human beings should aspire to is a knowledge of the infinite and eternal substance.

A year after my mother died, I started going to the Talmud Torah school. For the instruction in the first four forms, each of which lasted two years, no fee had to be paid; hence children from both rich and poor families attended and completed these school years. My teacher in the first form was Mordechai de Castro. In the first two years, we read the prayer book. In the next two years, Joseph de Faro taught us how to read the Torah in Hebrew. In the third form, Abraham Baruch instructed us in the translation of extracts from the Torah, and we also studied the interpretation of the Torah. In the following two years, Salom ben Joseph expounded on the books of the prophets.

One morning, when I was nine, and completing my first form in school, Father said that he was going to marry again. The name of the woman who came to our house and slept with Father in the same bed that Mother died in was Esther. She was a very silent woman: she had just arrived from Lisbon and had never learned a word of a language other than Portuguese, just as we never learned anything more about her life. It was her sister, Margrieta, who brought her to Amsterdam; she had lived in the city for a long time and sometimes visited Esther in our house. Whenever they were together, however, they spent their time in silence, as though they had nothing to say to each other. They were probably not too keen to evoke any memories from their past.

The school classes began at eight in the morning and continued until eleven, when the bell announced their end. Then we went home to eat and rest for a while; at two o'clock sharp we went back to school; in the evening we went to evening prayer at the synagogue to sing psalms. In the fifth form, Isaac Aboab instructed us in the Talmud; each day we studied a commandment from the Mishnah and the relevant commentary from the Gemara. In the two years of sixth form we studied the Gemara and the Tosafot, and the relevant commentaries made by Maimonides, with Saul Levi Mortera, the chief rabbi of the community.

When my elder brother, Isaac, died in September 1649, my father decided that I would not be able to complete my education as a rabbi, not only because he did not have enough money to pay for the instruction but also, and even more important, because someone had to help him manage the shop. So I, the boy who was groomed to become a rabbi, became a shop assistant in my father's shop. I continued, however, to study the Torah in communal schools where lectures were held once a week by some of the rabbis who had been my teachers in the Talmud Torah school. Rabbi Mortera taught in one of these schools, called "Keter Torah" (Crown of Law), while Rabbi Aboab gave regular lectures in another school called "Torah Or" (Law Is Light). My father felt somewhat guilty for not being able to provide for my education as a rabbi, and also because I had to help him with his work instead of going to school. He therefore asked Rabbi Menasseh ben Israel, the author of *The Hope of Israel,* to tutor me. My new teacher was different from the other rabbis: he had an excellent command of the Cabala and also of non-Jewish philosophy. He gave me a copy of *The Pre-Adamites* by the French Calvinist Isaac La Peyrère, in which he claimed that there had been human beings on earth even before Adam and Eve and that Moses had not written the Torah, but that it had been compiled by several men, and also that the world was actually much older than six thousand years. I later posed some questions arising out of my conversations with Rabbi Menasseh to Rabbi Mortera and Rabbi Aboab during their school lectures, and they were flabbergasted. I asked them whether our existence continued in completely the same form after our death, and they answered that our soul continued to live, whereas our body died. I then asked them whether our soul continued to exist in its entirety, that is, in the same form, and their answer was that the soul continued to exist in the same form, as the soul was indivisible. I then asked them if that meant that all fears, passions, and evil thoughts remained there, and the rabbis did not know how to answer my question, offering only some vague explanations. I soon stopped visiting Keter Torah and Torah Or, as it no longer interested me why, when someone sacrificed an ox or sheep for their salvation as a gift to God, the sacrificed animal was not supposed to have a defect; what interested me more was the nature of human beings and their role and place in nature. I was not too eager to know why only unleavened bread was supposed to be eaten seven days after Passover; I wanted to know what the link was between human beings and nature. It was of no great interest to me why, if two or more brothers lived together and one of them died without progeny, the wife of the deceased was supposed to marry her brother-in-law; I wanted to know if it was possible for human beings to achieve complete freedom, and to find the ways of actually achieving this.

In June 1650, my eldest sister, Miriam, married Samuel de Casseres, who studied as a rabbi under Rabbi Mortera. A year later, while giving birth to her son, Daniel, Miriam died, and Samuel married my younger sister, Rebecca.

My father's last wife, Esther, died in late October 1653, and five months later he too passed away.

From that moment on I was in charge of the shop, and Gabriel was my assistant. These were hard times for us; with every passing day fewer customers came to our shop, and one of the ships that was supposed to transport necessary merchandise was intercepted by pirates. That winter we had little food and there was not enough firewood. Yet I managed to elicit a strange kind of pleasure from that period of scarcity, probably because I had always had a dislike for handling money. I hated the contact that occurred between my fingers and the coins or paper printed with the various denominations. I preferred to handle them through the use of a handkerchief or tweezers, and I was somehow happy that I rarely had to touch them now.

The citizens of Amsterdam would never forget the second half of 1654 and the first half of 1655, when the plague was raging: seventeen thousand people died in ten months, every tenth person in the city. Amsterdam was closed off for several months; only a small portion of ordered goods managed to reach the city, and our shop was forced to close for several weeks. Having to think about survival did not take me away from my thoughts about God, existence, and the origins of passion: even as I sat in the corner of the shop, where no one came, for hours on end listening to the rumbling of my empty stomach, I assessed and reevaluated the differences between satiety and hunger, between greed and self-denial.

During the periods when there were enough customers and when there was no illness in the city, I thought that the work in the shop might distract me from my books until I turned into a shopkeeper who reads books before going to sleep. I tried to suppress that thought, as I considered science and thinking about God the only pleasures worth anything. I then forced myself to face the reality that I would probably remain a shopkeeper until the end of my days. I tried to reconcile myself to my certain future until, one evening, I met Franciscus van den Enden in front of our shop. It was the end of 1655, and I was just locking the door when I heard someone asking:

"Are you closing, sir?"

"Yes," I said, turning to the man who had asked the question and who was silhouetted by the street lanterns—I could not see his face, only the outline of his diminutive form and the hand he was scratching his bald head with—and who was tapping the pavement with his foot.

"I just wanted to buy some dried figs and wine."

"I'm sorry, sir, it's time for me to go home," I said in a weary voice.

"Young gentleman, right now I'm willing not only to offer you money for my dried figs and wine but also fifty verses of Ovid's *Metamorphoses* as well as the first act of Terence's *Eunuchus*." Noticing my confusion, he added, "And five letters by Seneca at that."

I smiled and opened the shop.

I spent that evening at Franciscus van den Enden's house. He was indeed an eccentric: as a young man he had joined the Jesuit order in Antwerp, where he was born, because, as he claimed, he was determined to spend his entire life in the devotion of God, rejecting all worldly pleasures. Two years after he had become a monk, he was thrown out of the monastic order as soon as the news spread of his frequent visits to the wife of a high military official when her husband was away fighting a war. Fearing that the belligerent husband might, upon his return from the battlefield, kill him, Franciscus, or Frans, as they called him, left the city and returned there two years later with a certificate from a Jesuit academy, armed with which he commenced teaching literature, Latin, and Greek in Antwerp. Earning the respect of the citizens of his native city, he was readmitted to the monastic order as a penitent, an event that was celebrated as the return of the prodigal son. Once more, however, since he was prone to the seduction of the wives and daughters of prominent people in Antwerp and, moreover, as he was in the habit of stealing money given by the faithful, he was defrocked. He again disappeared from the city for some time, but when he returned, he claimed that he had become a doctor of medicine. No one in the city, however, was able to tell where he had been awarded the title of doctor, as he himself admitted, irresistibly charming in his sincerity also revealing all his previous mischief. Franciscus healed the sick through his often bizarre recommendations. Only those who did not strictly adhere to these recommendations had any chance of staying alive. When he was forty, he married Clara Maria Vermeeren, and a year later, in 1643, they had a daughter, whom they named after her mother. Shortly after her birth, one of Franciscus's patients died from taking the doctor's advice to spend the winter night on the roof of his house as a cure for a cold, and the Van den Enden family had to move to Amsterdam. There they had two lots of twins, out of which only Adriana Clementina and Mariana survived. I had heard the story of Franciscus van den Enden's life many times; he enjoyed telling it and each time he told it in a different way. When I heard it for the first time that evening having gone to his house in the center of Amsterdam, I knew that we would become friends for life. It occurred to me, while I was listening to him recounting the follies of his life, that he was probably the only person at that moment in time from whom I wanted to learn something.

On that first evening of our acquaintanceship, a group of Franciscus's young friends had gathered in his house. He tutored them in Latin in order to support his family after failing to earn enough money from the gallery and bookshop on the ground floor of his house. After having retold his life story, which the others had heard many times before and so had taken to correcting him whenever he made any mistakes, either deliberately or accidentally, Franciscus began expounding on linguistics and then theology. He explained that faith in God was a totally personal choice and that it could not be guided by an institution of authority, and that true piety consisted of a deep love of God and of our fellow creatures, and that this was the love that formed the essence of the Torah and the books of the prophets, as well as the Gospels. With a red face and an even redder bald patch, he spoke about the love of God, passionately gesticulating with his hands, when a fair-haired little girl came into the room with eyes full of tears. They later told me it was his youngest daughter, Mariana.

"Jesus died, Father," said the girl, beginning to cry loudly, and jumped into her father's arms.

"You can't do anything about it, dear, such is life," he said, stroking her fair hair.

"But, Father, I want Jesus always to be with us," the little girl was barely able to utter the words through her tears.

"Even God can do nothing. Think about it, he was very old and all his teeth had fallen out; he couldn't even eat properly."

One of Franciscus's friends, noticing my confusion, explained to me that Jesus was the name of one of the dogs in the Van den Enden family.

The next day Franciscus began tutoring me in Latin, and we read Horace, Virgil, Ovid, and Petronius in his home. He often urged us not only to recite their works in the original but also to act them out. After the lessons we had talks about theology, literature, music, and philosophy, and through Franciscus, I became acquainted with the work of Francis Bacon, Giordano Bruno, Machiavelli, Hobbes, Thomas More, and René Descartes. In Franciscus's house I met Jarig Jellesz, who had previously worked as a merchant in spices and dried fruit; he later sold his shop and was now entirely dedicated to philosophy and theology. He introduced me to Jan Rieuwertsz, who managed a bookshop and printing works, and to Simon de Vries, who remained a friend until the end of my life.

Franciscus had less and less time to give me Latin lessons, since it was around this time that he began devoting himself to the study of Isaac the Blind's interpretations of the Talmud. His daughter Clara Maria often stood in for him; although she was only twelve, she had an excellent command of Latin, equal to that of her father's. She was born with her right leg somewhat shorter than her left, but when she walked, her limp was not easily discernible to the eye—only the ear could hear the different sound in her step. The eye could also notice a certain sluggishness, which is likely to have been aimed at slowing down the course of time. Franciscus had taught his daughter Dutch and French virtually from her birth; at five she started learning Latin, then English at six, and Spanish at seven. At the same time she studied the lute and harpsichord, and since her father owned a gallery, the painters who sold their art there also gave her lessons in drawing. I met her when she was twelve, and she had already been teaching Latin for a year. The first thing that struck me about her was her wonderful eyes. Her left eye displayed a kind of questioning amazement that emanated from the iris and seemed to make its way into the pupil. What her right eye imparted was omniscience: her gaze originated from deep behind her pupils; from there it spread to the iris and reached into the very heart of what she was looking at. In this way, the collocutor's gaze was absorbed into Clara Maria's left eye, which demanded an answer. The gaze of her right eye penetrated the eye of the collocutor and it was there that it found all the answers. She had no friends to keep her company while knitting or embroidering on the porch during the warm afternoons or in the house when it got cold. No, she had not dedicated her life to loneliness—she simply could not find girls in Amsterdam who would give her the answers to the questions she wanted to ask and who would ask the questions she would have wanted them to ask. When she was not giving Latin lessons, she read books while rocking back and forth in the rocking chair, talked to the fish in the aquarium in the corner of her room, or played the lute or the harpsichord, which bore the inscription *Musica laetitiae comes medicina dolorum* ("Music is the companion of joy and the remedy for suffering"). She sometimes left the house for hours and came back in the evening with pockets full of yellow leaves in autumn, or flowers in spring and summer. Her mother was worried about her daughter as a tarot fortune-teller had told her that her eldest daughter would marry a man whom she did not love and who did not love her, and with whom she would have no children. This state of anxiety ended when Clara Maria's mother died and the prediction was forgotten. Clara Maria always began her lessons in an unusual way: she would tell me in Latin about what she had dreamed the previous night.

The Rolling of Words

Have you ever dreamed of her, Spinoza? Have you ever seen her in your dreams? While she teaches you conjugations and declensions, while she pronounces words whose meanings are still unknown to you, does the way in which the sounds roll in her throat, becoming louder as they move upward toward her mouth and are articulated through her lips before reaching your ears, excite you? Have you ever dreamed of her making other sounds in her throat, calling you, or pronouncing your name, not only to warn you that that specific noun is not in the correct case, but sounds she may make when waking up or going to sleep? Have you ever had dreams of her whispering your name?

Dreaming and I

It is a curious thing, _____, but I stopped dreaming in my earliest childhood. The dreams of those who dream are stimulated by affections, and I have dedicated my life to the understanding of affections and ways of overcoming them.

Soon after Clara Maria began tutoring me in Latin her mother died. She showed no sign of sorrow, and I respected her even more for that. I respected her more for how she controlled her feelings than for the knowledge she commanded: I have always associated tears and suffering with people who were unable to hear the call of knowledge, who, instead of dedicating themselves to the discovery of the deepest truth, have surrendered themselves to affections. But one thing did change in Clara Maria after her mother died: she began leaving her home more often without telling Franciscus where she went, and she returned home only after many hours' absence.

One afternoon I joined Clara Maria. We came to the last house in the city, and then we went on even farther. The road led far away toward the horizon, and the clouds were scattered in the sky. I could hear our steps breaking the silence that was becoming thinner and thinner. In spite of limping, Clara Maria walked faster and faster, and I followed her. Then I could hear her repeating: "Who am I? Clara Maria. Who am I? Clara Maria. Who am I? Clara Maria. . . ." I heard her repeating the same question and giving the same answer as she walked faster and faster, limping all the time, and asking herself the same question and answering it at a faster and faster pace: "Who am I? Clara Maria. Who am I? Clara Maria. Who am I? Clara Maria. . . ." Then, exhausted from all the running, or from her questions and answers, she fell to the ground, but she continued asking herself and answering the same question: "Who am I? Clara Maria. . . ." The repeated questions and answers appeared to me to be some kind of self-torture, as though she was asking herself and giving the answer while someone was whipping her soul. Her eyes were closed; she had her eyelids tightly closed as though she were afraid of allowing something to escape from her pupils. Then she asked the same question several more times, "Who am I?" without uttering her name. She seemed to release a kind of painful exhalation instead, something resembling a mute shriek. I stood beside her body and watched her. Now she even stopped asking the question. The expression of torment on her face was suddenly replaced by an expression of indifference. Her eyes were still shut, but seamlessly—her eyelids now became completely relaxed. Her lips slowly spread in a smile; she half-opened her eyes and began staring at me with a strange look that went right through me, ending up some five steps behind me.

She said, "This is so strange. There is a moment when, if you ask yourself in a deep enough manner who you are and if you say your name earnestly enough, if you completely transform yourself into that question and that answer, you will forget your own name, probably because your name is the wrong answer to the question *Who am I?* And then you also forget the question. You will not even be able to find that *Who am I?* in your mind to ask the question, probably because with that question, with that *Who am I?*, you cannot reach your *I.* This is a wonderful moment, when you lose both the answer and the question: you have the feeling that you are also losing all those things that you believe constitute yourself, which they do not in reality. It is only then that you become yourself, it is then that you truly exist within yourself."

■ □ ■ □ ■

Don't you want to ask yourself who you are? Don't you want to repeat incessantly to yourself, *Who am I?* I can imagine you running in the meadows that begin where Amsterdam ends, while Clara Maria, still limping, is running after you, and you repeat the question and the answer alternately, at first in a monotonous way, like someone who takes off their shoes or washes their hands, then faster and faster, and then with some weariness, and then in a surprised tone, until you have finally lost both the question and the answer, until you have lost yourself in *Who am I?* finding yourself in your own name, finding your *I*.

■ □ ■ □ ■

Which *I*, _____?

What we call *I* is just based on the idea we have about our body and our soul, which react to the actions of other bodies and other souls. I heard and saw Clara Maria running and repeatedly stating the question and answer, *Who am I? Clara Maria,* and I was able to believe that it was I who saw and heard Clara Maria and was asking myself why she was doing what she did. I was also able to believe that it was I whom Clara Maria tutored in Latin, and that it was I who was excommunicated from the Jewish community, and also that it was I who was born one night in November. But which one of these *I*'s was indeed my *I*? None of them. This is because the perception of your *I* in a specific period of time and with regard to a limited number of specific things is the wrong understanding about your *I*. You can have a true understanding of your *I* only if you see your *I* without the influence exerted by questions and answers—such as *Who am I? Clara Maria,* stated by a thirteen-year-old girl—without the anger over your excommunication, without the embarrassment of your first day in school and your first visit to the synagogue, without the pain you felt when you were born. The true *I* appears only when you see your *I* without any outside influences exerted upon you, without any ideas, without any touch, sound, smell, taste, or sight, which have aroused your senses in the course of your life, when you see your *I* outside time and without any correlation between that *I* and any other, alien *I*'s: it is only then that you will know your true *I,* perceiving it in correlation to God—the eternal and infinite substance.

As far as Clara Maria's naive experiences are concerned, what she called the "true existence within you"—which occurred after she had forgotten the question *Who am I?*—was the result of sheer exhaustion.

Before long she got up and put her fingers on my cheeks.

"Feel how cold they are," she said.

■ □ ■ □ ■

Didn't you wish that this moment with Clara Maria had lasted forever, Spinoza? Her cold fingers on your cheeks. Until the end of time. And even beyond.

■ □ ■ □ ■

Every continuance comes to an end. Only substance, essences, and attributes are eternal.

Substance is that which is in itself and is conceived through itself. Substance is God—a being absolutely infinite: a substance consisting of an infinity of attributes, of which each one expresses an eternal and infinite essence. Substance equals God, God equals substance; there is no substance outside God, there is no God outside substance. Hence there is but a single substance (God), which is conceived through itself, which permeates all its parts, and, apart from that substance in all its modifications, or states, nothing else exists in the nature of things. Substance has an infinity of attributes and each one of them expresses its essence. Of this infinity of attributes we can comprehend only two: Thought and Extension. These two attributes are in constant association. An infinity of modes is derived from each attribute, which are in fact modifications, or states, of substance. Modes are individual things through which substance is manifested and are derived from attributes, just as attributes are derived from substance. Everything that is derived directly from substance and attributes is again infinite and eternal—as are the infinite and eternal modes: the mode of motion and rest comes from the attribute of Extension, the mode of the infinite intellect comes from the attribute of Thought, and the appearance of the entire universe comes from the encounter of these two attributes. The infinite and eternal mode of motion and rest is the sum total of all bodies, which are finite modes, and contains in itself all motion and rest. The infinite and eternal mode identified as the infinite intellect contains in itself all individual ideas. The infinite and eternal mode identified as the appearance of the entire universe contains in itself the wholeness of the world and is the sum total of the laws on the relationship between transient and finite modes. So, _____, we now come to transient and finite modes, whose number is countless, as opposed to eternal and infinite modes, of which there are only three; the number of transient and finite modes is equal to the number of transient and finite bodies in the world. Seen through the attribute of Extension, the modes are bodies; seen through the attribute of Thought, the modes are ideas. This is how the fall from perfection into imperfection takes place: attributes come from substance, eternal and infinite modes come from attributes, the countless transient and finite modes—bodies—come from eternal and infinite modes. Perfection is Creative Nature (*Natura naturans*), and that is substance and attributes; imperfection is Created Nature (*Natura naturata*), and that is modes. Creative Nature can be conceived only through itself; Created Nature can be conceived only through substance.

For however long that moment may be protracted, Clara Maria will one day have to take her freezing fingers from my cheeks. One day, not long after that moment, her fingers will exist no longer, and the same will happen to my cheeks. Hence only eternity is worthy of devoting our thoughts to.

■　□　■　□　■

The fact that her fingers and your cheeks are to disappear within such a brief period of time—this transience—isn't it more of a reason to pay attention to transient things, instead of devoting our lives to eternity, which, regardless of what transient beings may think, is eternal anyway? Don't you think it can be more meaningful to spend your life thinking about Clara Maria's fingers than thinking about the eternity of substance?

■ □ ■ □ ■

THREAD TWO

The Cherem

The name of the man who came that evening in April 1656 to Franciscus van den Enden's house was Accipiter Beagle. According to his account, he was born thirty-six years earlier in Macedonia, one of the provinces of the Ottoman Empire. The Turks were in the habit of taking children from their mothers in that region; they brought them to Istanbul, converted them to Islam, changed their names, and spoke to them in Turkish so that they would forget their mother tongue. Then they trained them to be the cruelest of warriors and sent them back to their native land to fight their own people. He could not remember how old he was when they took him from his home, but he thought he had not been older than five. In Istanbul he learned Turkish and forgot his native language, he was circumcised and studied the Koran, he relinquished his Orthodox Christian faith, he was given the name Mehmed, and he forgot the name his parents had given him. He remembered only two words from his mother tongue: *jastreb* (hawk), because of the bird he had tamed as a child, which used to land on his head and peck him with its beak, and *Bigla,* the name of the mountain on the slopes of which stood the village of his birth. The Turks trained him in how to handle a knife. He vigorously talked about his training: the group was first given corpses to butcher, and later they were brought to places where families had abandoned their ailing and older members. The Turks urged the young warriors to massacre the old and ailing in order to encourage bloodthirstiness. When he was not learning the ways of a warrior, a few inhabitants of Istanbul taught him the meaning of the words *love* and *passion.*

He was also taught of things beyond the senses. One of the younger warriors, who was himself of Slavic descent from Macedonia, secretly introduced him to a cabalist, Moshe ben Elochim, who lived on the coast of the Bosphorus, to tutor him in Hebrew, and who also spoke to him about the Zohar and Sefer Yetzira. When he was sixteen, he was sent to fight in one of the western territories of the empire; he arrived there with a group of warriors after riding for many days: from the start they burned villages, raped women, killed, and looted. One morning they attacked a mountain village, each of the warriors assaulting one house. While Accipiter Beagle (at that time his name was still Mehmed) watched the house he had set on fire burn, and while three corpses cooled down in the yard, a hawk landed on his head and pecked him. The young warrior immediately realized that he had killed his own mother and brothers. That night he killed the other warriors, and with the hawk on his head, set off to the south on horseback. From time to time the hawk flew in front of him, showing him the way to the sea. Riding through Macedonia, they finally came to Salonika. There he sold his horse since he needed the money to board a ship. One Thursday he, still with his hawk, found himself in Venice. There he became friends with some cabalists and studied Latin through Hebrew. He changed his name into Accipiter (*hawk* in Latin) Beagle (after the mountain on which he was born). While he was considering whether to stay in Venice for good, his hawk died, and he took this to be a sign that he should set sail again. He traveled to Leipzig, Paris, and London and became acquainted with the doctrines of the Rosicrucians and Freemasons. He also spoke about the unbelievable adventures he had had in all those cities, but there was something much more interesting about him than his life story. It was his teaching—apparently a mixture of the doctrines of the cabalists, Rosicrucians, and Freemasons, but at the same time very different. He claimed that there had been human beings even before Adam and Eve, which was not unusual—this was an idea also being extolled by all intelligent men who had no fear of religious fanatics—but, apart from that, Beagle argued that the first humans originated from apes. He convinced us that a careful comparison between the skeletons and organs of human beings and apes would lead anyone to the same conclusion. He maintained that God first created a single grain of matter and that everything came from that grain. The grain exploded, releasing enormous heat; driven by the explosion, matter expanded to the ultimate limits allowed by God, whereas during the contact between smaller bodies, invisible to the naked eye, larger and larger bodies were created. The expansion lasted for millions of years and when it ended, the created forms—the Earth and other celestial bodies—began to cool down. Accipiter Beagle left Amsterdam two days later, saying that he was leaving for the city where his teaching was needed most—Madrid, the heart of the Inquisition.

I was incredulous of Accipiter Beagle's claims, since I did not believe in anything that I could not analyze myself. Yet his ideas seemed interesting to me. I recounted them jokingly to my acquaintances during our conversations; they were truly flustered hearing such claims, and soon the rabbis were to learn about what I had said.

One morning Rabbi Mortera came to my shop and, instead of asking for his usual pepper, tobacco, or mustard seeds, he told me that he wanted to visit my house that evening. Judging from his voice, the twitching of his right eye, and the way in which he shut the door, I guessed what he wanted to talk about.

That evening he knocked at the door while I was looking at a drawing of an ape Clara Maria van den Enden had done. I had asked her to do that for me after Accipiter Beagle aroused my interest with his ideas about the origins of the human species. Clara Maria, who drew as well as she spoke foreign languages and played musical instruments, had drawn the ape in red pencil. The expression on the ape's face was reminiscent of an ill-tempered person, so that you could not tell whether it was a man with apelike features or an ape with the look of a human. As I knew it was Rabbi Mortera knocking on the door, I turned the drawing upside down and placed it on the table before I hurried to open the door.

"You know very well, Baruch, how much faith I had in you. You are not to become a rabbi only because your father didn't have enough money to pay for your education. Besides, your grandfather Abraham, your father's uncle, was my best friend," he said, twisting his beard between his thumb and index finger. "But during the last few weeks . . . I have heard strange things about you, Baruch."

"Strange?"

"They say you are proclaiming some ideas that do not agree with the Torah or with any of the scriptures of our sages and prophets."

"Yes, that's true," I said.

"I would like to hear it from your own mouth. What have you been saying to the young Jews here?"

"I tell them that there were people even before Adam and Eve, that God created only a grain of matter, and that everything was created of its own accord from that grain over the course of millions of years."

"So what you're saying is that the world was not created in seven days?" snarled the old man.

"It is not so easy to create a whole world," I replied.

"Baruch!" shouted Rabbi Mortera, pulling out a few hairs from his beard with his thumb and index finger. "You're certainly not claiming too, as some people have heard you say, that man was created from an ape!"

Then I took the drawing that was lying upside down on the table and placed it next to Rabbi Mortera's head.

"Look how similar you are," I said, looking alternately at the rabbi and the drawing. "Like brothers. How could anyone claim, after they have seen this, that man was created by God when it is obvious that he was created from an ape?"

Rabbi Mortera suddenly struck me hard on the cheek. The old man just turned and left the house, never again to come to my shop to buy mustard seeds, pepper, or tobacco.

A week later the Rabbinic Council decided to excommunicate me from the Jewish community, and a few days after the meeting of the council members, the decision was announced officially in the synagogue. My brother Gabriel later told me how the *cherem,* the act of my excommunication, was pronounced. The believers held lit black candles in their hands, while one of the rabbis opened the tabernacle, touching the holy books of the law. Then Rabbi Mortera read the text of the excommunication:

The lords of the *ma'mad,* having long known of the evil opinions and acts of Baruch de Spinoza, have endeavored, by various means and promises, to turn him from his evil ways. But having failed to make him mend his wicked ways and, on the contrary, daily receiving more and more serious information about the abominable heresies, which he practiced and taught, and about his monstrous deeds, and having for this numerous trustworthy witnesses who have deposed and borne witness to this effect in the presence of the said de Spinoza, they became convinced of the truth of this matter; and after all of this has been investigated in the presence of the honorable *chachamium,* they have decided, with their consent, that the said de Spinoza should be excommunicated and expelled from the people of Israel. By decree of the angels and by the command of the holy men, we excommunicate, expel, curse, and damn Baruch de Spinoza, with the consent of God, blessed be he, and with the consent of the entire holy congregation, and in front of these holy scrolls with the 613 precepts that are written therein; cursing him with the excommunication with which Joshua banned Jericho, and with the curse that Elisha cursed the boys, and with all the castigations that are written in the book of the law. Cursed be he by day and cursed be he by night; cursed be he when he lies down and cursed be he when he rises up. Cursed be he when he goes out and cursed be he when he comes in. The Lord will not spare him, but then the anger of the Lord and his jealousy shall smoke against that man, and all the curses that are written in this book shall lie upon him, and the Lord shall blot out his name from under heaven. And the Lord shall separate him unto evil out of all the tribes of Israel, according to all the curses of the covenant that are written in this book of the law. But you that cleave unto the Lord, your God, are alive every one of you this day. No one should communicate with him, neither in writing, nor accord him any favor, nor stay with him under the same roof, nor come within four cubits in his vicinity; nor shall he read any treatise composed or written by him.

I had known about the *cherem* sometime earlier, and I was prepared to leave the house I shared with my brother, as the *cherem* commanded that all my relatives sever all links with me. Upon leaving home I took some of my books, and the following day porters brought the rest of my books and the large red-canopied bed in which my mother gave birth to Isaac, myself, Rebecca, Miriam, and Gabriel, and in which both she and my father died. I moved to Franciscus van den Enden's house, who, as soon as the news had spread around Amsterdam that I might be excommunicated, offered me a place in his home if I were forced to leave mine. Someone told me that my name had been erased from the sign over our shop—BENTO

AND GABRIEL SPINOZA—but I never went back there to see this. Moreover, I never saw my brother again; eight years later someone told me that he had left for Barbados.

Samuel de Casseres came one evening to Franciscus van den Enden's house and said that he wanted to talk to me alone, adding that it was Rabbi Mortera who had sent him. The Jewish community knew all about my situation and expected me to show weakness and repent. They offered me a thousand guilders a year if I appeared in the synagogue and admitted that I had been wrong and asked for forgiveness. I told Samuel to let Rabbi Mortera know that I would never do as requested, not even for ten thousand guilders. Samuel told me that if I did not accept the proposal, Rabbi Mortera and Rabbi Aboab would demand from the authorities that I be banished from the city on the grounds that my claims were not only against Judaism but also against the Christian doctrine and that I could also corrupt young Christians. I asked Samuel to give my regards to Rabbi Mortera and to say that I wished him good health.

Although I refused to accept the thousand guilders, I actually needed them badly, although perhaps not at that precise moment, since I had a new home and I earned some money as a Hebrew and mathematics tutor. The real difficulty was that my home was not permanent and my earnings not sure. If the city authorities agreed to Rabbi Mortera's demand and expelled me from Amsterdam, I would not know where to go or what to do for a living. One evening I told Franciscus of my fears, and he, knowing about my love of telescopes and microscopes, told me that it could be useful if I learned how to grind and polish lenses, adding that he had a friend who could teach me the craft. I began by reading *Astronomy and Refraction* by Priest Scheiner, *De Vero Telescopi Inventore* by Borellius, and *Optics* by Descartes. My study of optics commenced with mathematical theory: I was interested in the angle at which lenses best refracted the rays of light and brought them into focus. Later, with the help of Franciscus's friend, Jan Glazemaker, I learned how to manufacture lenses: First, using a blade coated with a mixture of ashes and oil, a piece of glass is cut. The lens is then firmly fixed in tar while the centering axis and the mill roughly shape the radii and angles. Fine grinding is the next phase in order to obtain accurate angles and radii. Finally, abrasives and polishing powder are applied to finish the lenses.

One Thursday, Francisco Monros, a friend of Franciscus from Madrid who studied the flight of insects, visited his home. He told us that he had met Accipiter Beagle, who had arrived in Spain a few months earlier. Beagle had already started writing down his claims about the origins of the human species and the creation of the world, hoping to publish them one day, believing that he could sway people's beliefs away from religious dogma and crush the power of the Inquisition. A few days later Francisco Monros left Amsterdam, having recorded in detail the flight of a type of butterfly that, so he claimed, lived only in that area. Just a day or two before his departure, we received the news of Accipiter Beagle's end. The Inquisition Tribunal burned him at the stake one day in Madrid, having found, in a printing works, copies of two books entitled *From Ape to Adam* and *A Brief History of Time,* written by him. Meanwhile, I gave up speaking about Accipiter Beagle's ideas concerning the origins of the human species and the creation of the world, which I had earlier recounted in rather a casual manner to some of my acquaintances.

When the rabbis' threats to have the city authorities expel me from Amsterdam became more persistent—all this with the aim of making me repent—I knew that it was time for me to leave. Albert Burgh, another of Franciscus's Latin students, promised to find a new home for me. His father, Conraad Burgh, was a magistrate and one of the richest men in Amsterdam. They offered me one of their houses, in a village close to Amsterdam. The cemetery of the Amsterdam Jews, where Hanna Deborah and Michael Spinoza were buried, was near the village. Toward the end of 1659, I moved into this village called Ouderkerke, where the air was as light as a seagull's feather.

I remember the night before I left Amsterdam. Only Clara Maria and I were in the house. She expected her father and sisters to return from Antwerp, where they had been visiting their cousins, the following morning. Clara Maria played the lute in the next room while I was trying to control my anger and fear. From time to time I realized that I was clenching my fists and then releasing them again.

Carrying Air

Can you imagine her, Spinoza? Can you imagine yourself approaching her while her eyes are trying to avoid your pupils? While she is breathing and gasping for air a little, can you imagine yourself beginning to undress her slowly? She pauses between breathing in and breathing out, between breathing out and breathing in, as if she is carrying the air to some unknown place. Then, while you quickly undress, can you imagine placing her under your body and feeling the warmth of her thighs? Can you imagine yourself slowly going into her? Does your fantasy end here, while your hand is making a last movement on your penis as you spill your semen?

Drawing Air

I was lying on the red-canopied bed. My fingers were clenched into a fist. I could hardly breathe, I was struggling to draw air into my nostrils. I was supposed to leave Amsterdam, but I did not know what to do next.

Clara Maria played the lute in the next room.

Different

But everything might have been different, Spinoza. Let us suppose that you have been imagining something and that you are now lying with your belly wet from your semen. Let us imagine that you hear steps and that someone knocks at the door. The door opens and Clara Maria comes into the room.

"I can't sleep," she would say. "It's a full moon."

You take the blanket away from your body and sit on the bed. She asks you if you, too, cannot sleep when the moon is full, and you say that you cannot sleep at all. She wants to light a candle, and you are afraid that she might see your belly covered in semen, and you tell her that the light of the full moon is enough. She sits close to you on your bed. You are silent, you can hear her breathing, Spinoza, and you ask yourself whether she, too, can hear your breathing, or whether her thoughts are soaring, imagining, and picturing events that may one day happen.

You are both quiet; you can hear her breathing as she seems to be gasping for air a little. You might feel ashamed, Spinoza, but you should think yourself lucky that it is nighttime and that the candle is not lit, so that Clara Maria cannot see you blush. You are aware that she has smelled something. She might not say anything, she may remain silent, or she might say: "There is a strange smell in here," and you believe that she has never before smelled semen and that she cannot tell what that smell is. What would you say then, Spinoza?

Would you say: "It is the smell of semen"? Then she would blush; she would try to remember what she had read about semen, masturbation, and sexual intercourse in *On Bodily Fluids* by Blossomius. She would look at you in embarrassment, asking herself what you were fantasizing about a few moments before she came into the room. She might get up and run out of your room and lock herself in her room, listening to her heart pounding in her chest, while her disgust with the physical and her yearning for it would wage a fierce war inside her. She would probably not fall asleep that night. She would lie in bed with the blanket pulled over her head, tightly holding on to it as if someone was about to take it away from her.

But it might be different, it might be very different. Once she has smelled that strange smell, she might move her head closer to you and say: "It is you who smells like this. A strange smell indeed." And then, without waiting for you to tell her what the strange smell is, Clara Maria might come over to your bed and lean on the wall.

"How much can you learn about something new through smell?" Clara Maria might then ask you.

Trace and Essence

You can learn nothing through smell. For you can learn nothing through sensory experience. We can learn nothing through our senses, for as long as we try to grasp the essence of something through our senses, we only perceive the effect of that something on our body. This is not true knowledge—it is only the perception of an imprint, a mere trace of the physical upon the physical. A perception received through the senses is never the essence of something—it is only its appearance.

Smell

Why would you say that, Spinoza? Why? You could tell her that it is precisely through those traces, those imprints, that the essence of things can be understood and comprehended, that it is through them that one can grasp the substance.

Yes, Spinoza, why wouldn't you tell her that it is through the senses that we receive true knowledge? "Yes, Clara Maria," you'd say to her, "you can learn a part of the essence of things through smell."

Then Clara Maria would come nearer to you, smell your hair, move her nose close to your shoulder, take your hand, and smell your fingers.

"What about the rest of the essence of things? How could one learn about the rest of the essence of things?"

Knowledge

We can understand things in two ways: we can either understand them in their correlation to a specific time and place, or understand them as being part of God originating from the determination of divine nature. It is only in the second way that we can truly understand things: then we can understand them from the perspective of eternity, as their ideas contain the eternal and infinite divine essence within themselves. Our soul is an idea itself; it is but a modification of God in the attribute of Thought, just as our body is the modification of God in the attribute of Extension. The goal is to start from the soul and the body, which are merely modifications, and arrive, through the attributes, to the idea about them in God, to the pure essence itself. Hence we should proceed from the first type of knowledge, which is imperfect, to the second, and later to the third type of knowledge.

The Senses

No, Spinoza, forget about the attributes, substance, and essence; forget about the types of knowledge. Just look into her eyes, let your eyes meet in the semidarkness, and tell her that the remainder of the essence of things can be revealed through sight. Then take her head between your hands, take her closer to the window, where the moonlight is brighter, and then look at each other for a long time. Look at each other's pupils for a long time and feel how sweet those transient moments are, Spinoza—her very look changes from moment to moment, it is lost with the passing of every minute, it is not the same following each blink of the eye, always different and yet always hers. Look at her nostrils, see how she inhales and exhales, how her breasts go up and down, experience this transience, Spinoza, allow yourself to feel the pain of this transient world.

Then she might ask you:

"What about the rest of the essence? How can you learn about the rest of the essence of things?"

"Through sound," you might say, but you might also hold your answer back. You might show her the answer, you might utter "Ah" and again "Ah," both listening to the sound with your eyes closed. And she might take your hand, place the pulsating artery of your wrist on her ear, and listen to the flow of your blood.

"It throbs like the heart," she might say.

You might take her head and place it on the left side of your chest, where the sound of your heartbeat is the strongest, and then you might place your head on her left breast. You would remain still for some time, listening to each other's heart, to the flow of blood, to the pulsation of life.

"What next? How can you learn about other things?"

"Through taste," you would say, and you would slowly take her fingers, put them in your mouth, feel the trembling of her body, pass your tongue over her closed eyes. When you kiss her, she would believe that she now knew you by the taste of your mouth, her body melting. You would wait for her to ask you how you can fully get to the essence of things, but she would remain in a daze, she would continue living in that kiss as though it was her last glimpse of the house of her childhood before leaving it forever.

"Through touch," you would say, taking your lips away from hers.

"What do you mean, through touch?" she would ask you, letting her words drift slowly from her mouth.

"It is the last phase of the sensory knowledge of things," you would say and, touching yourself, you would take your clothes off bit by bit. With gentle caresses you would take her clothes off too, and then you would come to reveal the harmony of your bodies in both motion and rest, in tension and repose, in contortion and relaxation, in pain and contentment.

You would lie together that night on the bed, looking at how the silver moonlight was transformed into the purple light of dawn. Clara Maria would ask you if there was anything beyond sensory knowledge, and you would tell her about clear and distinct ideas, and about adequate ideas. You would explain to her the three types of knowledge, but you would not define them in a hierarchical manner, because,

Spinoza, if you truly aspire to attain something eternal and infinite—something where neither time nor space exists—if you strive to get to a realm without a spatial dimension, then how can you grade things, how can you put one type of knowledge before another, how can you put one type of knowledge below another type of knowledge?

What do you think would happen then, Spinoza? Would you leave Amsterdam? You would perhaps never come back, frightened at what you had done, frightened at what might have followed the action you incited, preferring to lose straightaway what you would inevitably have to lose one day, as all of it was transient and not eternal. You would perhaps not even think of her, nor would you think of what Clara was thinking at that moment. You would leave, while she remained standing at the window, thinking how easy it is for someone to forget and how difficult it is for others to do the same. Or you would leave Amsterdam and come back from time to time to see her, when her father was away. Then perhaps you would spend the night with Clara Maria, discovering ever new sounds, touches, tastes, forms, smells. . . .

■ □ ■ □ ■

Do you really believe that I would surrender myself to transient things perceived through the senses?

■ □ ■ □ ■

But does it really matter, Spinoza, does it really matter if those things are transient? Why should we spend our own transience thinking about eternal things (they are eternal anyway) and not take advantage of transient things, which need to be paid great attention to, to be watched over and nourished, as they are being born and die at each and every moment? Why should you yearn for the knowledge of substance and essence, and for the purpose of that knowledge—knowledge of something that exists independent of you anyway—and miss, for example, a slight change in Clara Maria's smile? Why should you yearn to know how substance is expressed in attributes, instead of yearning to know what Clara Maria's questions really mean? Why should you futilely strive toward the eternal and infinite, when you could try and experience the pulsation of finite and transient things, however brief this may be?

■ □ ■ □ ■

It is because the more knowledge of eternal things the soul embraces, the more of this knowledge remains within the soul. The more adequate ideas there are in the mind, the more of this particular mind remains within the divine attribute of Thought after the death of the body.

■ □ ■ □ ■

But why would you not believe that it is the imprint of transient things that continues to exist, that what returns to substance from ourselves, from its modifications, is not how we perceive substance, but the traces of transient things on our soul: someone's look that penetrates deeply into our pupils and then bumps on the ground astounded by its own power of insight?

You could find out that embracing transient things, reconciling yourself to the fact that we can only have and associate ourselves with transient things, is a fairly simple process, as simple as drinking a glass of water or jumping into one of Amsterdam's canals with a stone tied around your neck. You could both sit in different corners of the room; one of you could sit quietly, and the other could guess the thoughts of the one who remains silent—you could be surprised to learn how short the lives of thoughts are. You could both look into the endless sky (is it truly endless?) and search for stars that bear a resemblance to you: you could discover places for yourselves in the different constellations.

I can imagine you surrendering to transient things: you are both standing, Clara Maria and you; you stare at the clouds passing in the sky, forming short-lived shapes, melting into each other, or disappearing. I can see both of you creating transient things; I can see you one night impregnating Clara Maria. I can see you taking care of your son; you are close to him as he takes his first steps; later you explain to him the meaning of the words transient and eternal. You will be baffled to notice that you started by trying to explain to him the meaning of transience, which took much longer and gave you greater pleasure than the explanation of eternity.

I can imagine you learning to be happy with transient things, no longer afraid of their transience. I can see Clara Maria and you, gray haired, walking through the narrow streets of Italian cities with slow, unsure steps. You are looking at houses with paint peeling off (an orange house with carob trees in Florence reminds you of your home). I can see you both sitting on a bench somewhere in Rome, the Eternal City. After a while you bend to pick a yellow flower and give it to Clara Maria. She takes it in her hand. You both look at how the flower is beginning to wither—you are both happy, appreciating its transient beauty.

How different your life could have been if only you had accepted that it was possible to gain real knowledge through the senses, after she had come to your room.

■ □ ■ □ ■

But she did not come to my room.

The next day I left Amsterdam. I moved to Ouderkerke.

There I began my *Treatise on the Correction of the Understanding* (*Tractatus de Intellectus Emendatione*), which I left half-finished to dedicate myself to the writing of the *Short Treatise on God, Man, and His Well-Being;* however, I never returned to the writing of the former. What interested me most at that time was finding an answer to the question of what is truly good for a human being and the possibility of achieving it. Since man is an animal that differs from other animals only in that he has an intellect, that is, by being a reasoning animal, I knew that that good was to be found in knowledge. I wanted to get to the essence of things: I wanted to know what things actually were, how they existed, and why they existed as they did.

At the beginning of the summer of 1661, I moved to Rijnsburg, to a house situated at the far end of the village and where a certain Herman Hooman already lived. He was a chemist, and a Collegian as well. I set up my lens-manufacturing equipment in one of the back rooms. Both Ouderkerke and Rijnsburg looked like places where time had stopped. Sometimes, when the fog set in, they appeared totally forgotten by time.

I walked alone looking at the ground, and only the flight of a wild duck would remind me that there was also a world outside myself.

A few friends visited me from time to time, and I also tutored young students of philosophy. One of them was Johannes Casearius, who was ten years younger than me: he was born in Amsterdam in 1642 and, at the time, studied philosophy in Leiden. At first he came twice a week from Leiden to take lessons in Cartesian philosophy, but later he moved into the same house as me in Rijnsburg. In the lectures I gave to him I concentrated on the second and third sections of the *Principles of Philosophy* by René Descartes. The young man was obviously not too interested in philosophy: among all the postulates, definitions, axioms, and propositions propounded by Descartes, Johannes was most interested in his theory on the movement of comets. The fact that I gave daily lessons to this young man and that he lived in the same house as me was beginning to cause me some trouble, triggering a kind of intellectual jealousy among my friends. They could not stand the idea that Johannes had the opportunity of listening to my lectures every day. They tried to persuade me that the young man should leave the house I occupied as soon as possible. They even did this in some of the letters they sent me. I, in turn, sent them parts of my *Ethics,* and they informed me of how my doctrines were accepted and understood by them. Simon de Vries wrote to me:

As for our group, the procedure is as follows. One member (each has his turn) does the reading, explains how he understands it. Then if it should happen that we cannot satisfy one another, we have deemed it worthwhile to make a note of it and to write to you so that, if possible, it may be made clearer to us. Fortunate, indeed most fortunate, is your companion, Casearius, who lives under the same roof with you and can talk to you about the most important matters at breakfast, at dinner, and on your walks together. But although we are physically so far apart, you have frequently been present in my thoughts, especially when I am immersed in your writings and hold them in my hand.
Yours,
Simon de Vries.

I immediately wrote back to Simon.

My worthy friend,

I have received your letter, long looked for, for which, and for your cordial feelings toward me, accept my warmest thanks. Your long absence has been no less regretted by me than by you, but at any rate I am glad that my late-night studies are of use to you and our friends, for in this way I talk with you while we are apart. There is no need for you to envy Casearius. No one is more troublesome to me, and there is no one with whom I have to be more on my guard. So I should like to warn you and all our friends not to communicate my views to him until he has reached greater maturity. He is still too childish and unstable, more anxious for novelty than for truth. I hope, however, that in a few years he will correct these youthful faults. Indeed, as far as I can judge from his native ability, I am almost certain that he will. So his talent induces me to like him.

Yours,

B.

The next day, however, I told Johannes Casearius that I had no further plans to give him any more lectures on Descartes and that it was time for him to continue his studies in Leiden.

Form

Is this fear, Spinoza?

I can imagine Johannes coming into your room. He may tell you that he could not sleep, and he would sit on the chair next to your bed. You cannot see his face; the moonlight is coming from behind him, but he can see your face quite clearly. He may tell you that he wanted to ask you something and then he might pause. You might try to guess what he wanted to ask you before even hearing his question. You would think that he was about to ask you something that would make you blush: he might ask you something about tangible things. Soon you would find yourself describing to him the differences between form and matter, explaining that form is a limitation and that limitation is a negation. He asks you if that means that the body is also a negation, and you answer him that, in itself, the body is a negation, but that the body and the soul together form an individual entity and that the human soul is the very idea of the human body in God.

"But isn't the human body an idea in God as well?"

"No. I have already told you: the human soul is the very idea of the human body in God."

"So the body does not exist in God? Is it a negation for this reason?"

"I would like to think about that," you would say. "I cannot answer your question right away. For now I can only tell you that a negation is something that limits or is limited. The body is a negation, because it is not infinite."

"So I should wish that my body be infinite so that it wouldn't be a negation, shouldn't I?"

You would burst out laughing.

"I think you tend to oversimplify things."

"So what should I do if I don't want my body to be a negation?"

"The body is a form; the body cannot turn into formlessness. Losing its form, the body ceases to be a body. It thus follows that the body is a negation as long as it exists. It is impossible for the body to be infinite."

"So how can we attain infinity?"

"Through our reason."

Then you would speak to him about the three types of knowledge, but he would understand nothing.

"My reason gives me enjoyment. I enjoy infinity."

"What about finite, limited bodies?"

"No. I only enjoy infinity."

"And you never wish that your body would give you enjoyment?"

"No," you would say. "The body is not infinite."

"But let us imagine it were. Let us imagine that bodies were infinite. Even if they were not, why should we miss enjoying the body and the enjoyment it proffers?"

"I've already told you, I enjoy only infinity."

"But if the body and the soul form the same individual entity, and if a part of the soul is infinite, then the body, too, must possess an element of infinity."

"Infinite is that part of the soul that is dedicated to the knowledge of infinite things. The body cannot acquire such knowledge—the body is limited."

"But why shouldn't you examine the limitations of the body before getting to understand the infinity of the soul?"

You would remain speechless.

"Why would you have only indications of those limitations when you could have firsthand knowledge of the limitations themselves: why would you masturbate if you could make love?"

I would like to see you at a moment like this, Spinoza. I suppose that the limited parts of your body are about to reach a turning point. A change is also taking place in your infinite part: you start to breathe faster, the blood in your body is circulating faster, and everything around you is different, Spinoza. Even the wall does not look the same anymore.

"Lie down," he would say to you, and you would lie down, surprised at what you are now doing. "Now imagine for a moment that you are dead, that you no longer exist"—and he would begin to take your clothes off. "I really can't tell you what part of you should no longer exist and what part you should have to think no longer exists: whether it is your body or your reason." You would lie naked on the large red-canopied bed, on the bed in which you were conceived, in which you were born, and in which you would one day die. You would look at Johannes Casearius undressing and then standing naked in the moonlight. "If you want to experience your limitations, then forget about reason: experience the body and nothing else. Imagine that you only have this dead body and that it is your reason that has disappeared. But if you want to experience infinity, then forget that you have a body, think that the body, once it is dead, is no longer there and that reason is what continues to exist. Both things are possible if you imagine that you are dead. The most important thing is to imagine that you are dead, Spinoza," he would say and then lie on top of you. Then, under the weight of his body, you would feel as if you were truly dying, as if a part of you were dying, that part that had decided to spend its life thinking about life and not living it. As you are feeling the most hidden parts of his body inside you, you feel how the Spinoza devoted to permanent things is dying. Once you have felt your body more intensely than ever before, memories will pour out of you together with your scream: memories of death, of a certain death that took place in this bed many years before, when you felt it was the end of . . .

Grinding

I believe this is enough, _____! I believe there is no reason for you to go on with your assumptions. It is time for me to tell you what really happened in Rijnsburg.

After 1663, I rarely visited Franciscus van den Enden and I never slept in his house, as he wrote pamphlets in which he demanded the reorganization of authority. Although he never signed his pamphlets, everybody knew who their author was, so it was not only he and his family that fell under suspicion but also his friends. In his pamphlets he demanded a free society and political reform; he initiated petitions in which he insisted that the citizens of the other part of the Netherlands, the province of New Netherland—established on the continent across the Atlantic Ocean—be exempt from taxes. At the same time he wrote and published a Constitution of New Netherland, containing 117 articles, which was said to have provoked the anger of the Dutch government. In his pamphlet *Liberal Political Propositions and Considerations of a State,* he proposed that the government be elected by the people and was to include members of the ordinary strata of society, suggesting that "fishermen and prostitutes could best take care of the state economy."

In the spring of 1663, I moved from Rijnsburg to Voorburg, a village in the vicinity of The Hague. I lived in the house of the painter Daniel Tydeman on Kerkstraat. My room was on the upper floor and had a balcony. Opposite the house there was a church, and from a window at the back you could see the port, just across from the marketplace. At that time, my main income, if you exclude the financial assistance I received from my friends and the small sum I earned from tutoring—which was not even enough to pay my barber or buy a little tobacco—came from grinding lenses. I ate less and less food: one day I would have milk and butter soup and drink a mug of beer, and the next I had mush with raisins and butter. Every month I drank two pints of wine, and I spent a substantial sum on tobacco.

I often went to Amsterdam to see Simon de Vries, and Simon came to Voorburg even more often, especially after his mother and brother had died of the plague in May and June 1664. In the spring of 1665, I visited Simon in Amsterdam, where I fell ill with fever. After I got back to Voorburg, I bled myself several times hoping to be healed, but it did not help. Then I took a medicine that was prepared by mixing equal amounts of rosebuds and sugar, which were then boiled in water until a thick mass was obtained. I soon recovered from the fever. I will never know if it was because of the medicine or because the fever abated by itself.

That same year, I completed "On the Origin and Nature of Affections," the third part of the book I intended to call *Philosophy*, but which I later renamed *Ethics*. I sent this part to my friends, just as I had sent them the previous two, and then I put the work on this book aside. Thus I was able to dedicate myself fully to the material I had prepared for my *Theological-Political Treatise* (*Tractatus Theologico-Politicus*).

Simon de Vries died in September 1667. Shortly before his death, he demanded that I accept being the sole heir to his inheritance. I refused, as he had a sister who definitely needed his possessions more than I did. In his will he left me five hundred guilders. I only took three hundred, a sum I considered enough for me.

When I completed the *Theological-Political Treatise* and sent it to the printer, I left Voorburg and moved to The Hague, where I continued working on my *Ethics*. I rented a room in the attic of a house owned by a widow, Van der Werve, near the coast in a place they called Silent Harbor.

The *Theological-Political Treatise* was published anonymously, showing neither the name of the author nor the publisher. Jacob Thomasius, a theology professor from Leipzig, called the unidentified author "the emissary of Satan," and Regnier Mansveld, a professor from Utrecht, said that "the antichrist was born, since only he could be the author of such a work." Johannes Bredenburg from Rotterdam wrote a whole book opposing the *Theological-Political Treatise,* attacking its fatalism and its goal—allegedly, the spread of atheism. In the summer of 1670, the Court of the Reformed Church of Amsterdam sent to the general synod a warning demanding that the distribution and dissemination of this "dangerous and godless book" be banned. Shortly afterward, the regional synod of the city of The Hague sent a similar appeal to the general synod. By the end of the summer, the delegates of all synods concluded that "the most satanic and most blasphemous book that has ever appeared in the world must be banned," demanding that the book be burned. The Dutch Court sent a request to the state authorities, urging them to ban the sale of the book, find the author, and imprison him.

In February 1671, Clara Maria van den Enden married Theodor Kerckrinck.

When I was living in Franciscus van den Enden's house, I had tutored Theodor in mathematics. He was born in 1639 in Hamburg, where his father had been sent to study the martial arts of German soldiers. When I met him, he was living with his parents on the Keizersgracht in Amsterdam. Later, he studied medicine at the University of Leiden, and during his studies he wrote a tractate on alchemy, which he gave me to read before publishing it. Even though everybody who had read the tractate told him that he needed to prove his claim that by mixing antimony and mercury under specific circumstances you could obtain gold, he decided to go ahead and publish his work. Later on, his sole interest lay in the study of the human body. To this end he bought two microscopes from me, both of which were of my fabrication. He was particularly interested in the female genitalia: he refuted all previous misconceptions, dating back to the earliest of times, in his work entitled *Observations*. He always waited with impatience for a female criminal to be executed: the next day he would rush to the Anatomy Theater and dissect the body before the eyes of the curious observers. Instead of examining veins or the intestines like other surgeons, Theodor was entirely focused on the study of the female reproductive organs.

Later, in May 1671, I moved to the outskirts of the city, to a house on the Paviljoensgracht. I rented a room on the first floor of a house owned by the painter Hendrik van der Spyck (Spijk). He and his wife, Margareta, had three children at the time and were later to have another four.

In the summer of 1672, when the French army launched an assault on Dutch territories, and after Utrecht had fallen to the French, a French spy came to Hendrik van der Spyck's house, bringing me a letter written by Louis XIV. The French king demanded that I go with the man who had delivered the letter who would take me to him in Utrecht.

The Sun King, as they said he called himself, made a marked impression on me: while he was talking, he twisted his lips in an odd sort of way; he wore a wig and was constantly touching his hair; he had more powder on his face than he had probably seen gunpowder in the territories he had conquered.

"My dear Zbinoza, I'd like you to be my new Molière, my new Racine," he said, gesticulating with his arms while walking along the corridors of the castle in which, shortly before the defeat of Utrecht, lived the richest family in the city. Then he turned to me, obviously perplexed by my reticence. He pouted and asked me: "You know who Molière and Racine are, don't you?"

"Of course, but I am a philosopher, and they are playwrights."

"But it is high time I had a philosopher at my court, dear Zbinotsa."

"Spinoza," I corrected him.

"That's right, Spinoza," he said, nodding his head, while his wig quivered like the branches of trees shaken by children gathering fruit. "So, just as Racine and Molière live at my court, I would like you to live there too. Indeed, I need a wise man there, a wise man like you, dear Shpinoza, a philosopher no less, who would speak about God, about the most sublime things, and about me, of course. Ah, Zhbinoza, it would be wonderful if you could write a book about me." He looked at me, and in reply to the expression of my face, he added: "No, not only about me, it could be a book about myself and God, Zhbinoza."

"Your Majesty, I have to tell you that I am regarded as a blasphemer here: they have proclaimed me an antichrist and the messenger of Satan. If I do write a book about you and God, people will think I have written a book about you and Satan."

"Dear Shpinoza, you are so clever!" Saying this, he turned toward an open door down the corridor and shouted: "Jean! J-e-a-n! Bring me my pot!"

One of Louis' servants ran toward us.

"At your service, Your Majesty," he said, placing the chamber pot on the ground.

"I must fulfill a duty," said the king. He threw his cape back, bent forward, taking his trousers off, and sat on the chamber pot. "I can't stand your food," the king said, groaning. "I'm constipated all the time." Then his face twitched with pain, reddening due to the strain. "So you are saying it'd be inappropriate for you to write a book about me and God."

"No, Your Majesty, it is quite appropriate to write a book about you and God, but it would be inappropriate if I wrote that book. I would be comparing you to God, but since many people believe that I am the messenger of Satan, people might think that you have the characteristics of Satan, and not of God," I said, looking at the puffed-up face that was making one last effort.

"Oooh," sighed His Majesty with relief, and an expression of bliss appeared on his face. In a matter of seconds, he got up and pulled up his trousers.

The servant took the pot and disappeared down the corridor with it while we continued our walk.

"Well, if you write a book that you'd dedicate to me . . . it doesn't necessarily have to be about me. You can write whatever you wish, just dedicate the book to me. Then you can live at my court until the end of your life. In opulence, dear Shpinoza—the most beautiful maids of honor will be around you all the time, you'll eat only the best food, a servant will run after you with a chamber pot, you'll live a wonderful life—you just have to dedicate a book to me and . . . there you are, you're welcome at my court."

"I already have enough enemies at your court because of what I've written so far, I presume, and I really don't think it's a place where I'd feel very comfortable."

All of a sudden His Majesty stopped and began sniffing like a dog.

"Do I smell?" he asked me looking like the world was about to end.

"Yes, you do," I replied.

"Oh, no!" he said, making a sad face.

"What's wrong with that?"

"What do you mean, what's wrong? What do I smell of?"

"Of many things. You obviously use different perfumes. Both flagrantly and fragrantly," I said and smiled.

"You're a philosopher, there's no doubt about it. But do you think I'd ever ask you if I smelled of perfumes? I want to know if I smell unpleasant."

"No, not at all."

"You know, I'm afraid of taking a bath. I'm afraid of taking a bath just as much as I'm afraid of losing a battle," he said, putting his hand on his chest and throwing his head back, risking the wig falling off. I wondered how this could be true with the man who was, bit by bit, conquering Europe. "Dear Shpinoza, I never take a bath, but I change my underwear five times a day." He sniffed himself under his arms and then bent over and smelled himself between his legs.

"Yes, I smell, dear friend, I do smell after all. And in half an hour I'm supposed to meet one of my counselors who has just arrived from Paris. He might spread gossip later, saying that Louis, the Sun King, smells! Or rather, as you philosophers would put it, that I stink! That would be dreadful, dear Shpinoza, it would be the end of the world! I must change my apparel immediately," he said and ran in his high-heel shoes down the corridor. When he came to the end, he turned and, before vanishing through the door, shouted in his shrill voice:

"Think about it anyway, think about writing a book about me and God!"

I stayed in Utrecht a few more days and His Majesty received me on two other occasions. I was curious and asked him why he waged his wars—whether he was driven by hatred or greed—but he refused to tell me anything about his battles. He only showed interest in conversing about food, clothes, beautiful women, wigs, and perfumes. And, of course, he hoped to persuade me to write a book about him, or at least a book dedicated to him. It was more or less obvious that he waged his wars motivated by greed. He was not the one who actually led the battles: only the idea of war was his, not the method of waging it, just as it was his idea to find a wise man to mention him in a book. It must have been some of his counselors who had recommended me, for I remained Zbinoza, Shpinoza, or Zhbinoza to the Sun King.

Upon my return to The Hague, I found out that the news of my journey to Utrecht and my meeting with Louis XIV had already spread throughout the city. From the street beneath the window next to my bed I could hear passersby calling me a traitor and shouting out that I should be killed. Hendrik and Margareta were afraid that gangs of people would storm the house and create chaos, frightening or even hurting their children. I told them I would come if anyone knocked at their door. The following day, early in the morning, someone knocked at the door. I knew that Hendrik and Margareta were terrified, and I hurried to open the door. It was the old milk woman who had brought us milk.

A few days later, I learned that Franciscus van den Enden had left for Utrecht to offer his services to Louis, the Sun King, and persuade him to allow him to work at his court. In early autumn, I also learned that Franciscus had left for France. Two years later, one November afternoon in 1674, I heard that he had been sentenced to death for plotting against the Sun King.

From time to time I went to Amsterdam to meet my friends Jarig Jellesz, Pieter van Gent, Tschirnhaus, and Schuller, who gathered together every Tuesday and Thursday in Rieuwertsz's bookshop to take part in long discussions. One evening when I was in their company, I learned that the *Theological-Political Treatise* had been banned, together with several other books, including *Leviathan* by Thomas Hobbes. Some books appeared later in Rieuwertsz's bookshop that refuted my claims about God, but I could not reply to these attacks, as I wanted to complete my *Ethics*. I revised its third part and realized that it had to be divided into two additional parts. Apart from this, I began writing a Hebrew grammar book.

One warm day in July 1675, I went to Amsterdam and I gave the complete text of my *Ethics* to Rieuwertsz, hesitant as to whether to remain anonymous again or to put my name on its cover. I stayed for two weeks in Amsterdam until the printing of my book had to be suspended. Some theologians visited the Dutch prince, having heard the rumors that a book was in print in which I attempted to prove that God did not exist. Many people wrote attacking me; only Mariet Meester, the only woman in the Netherlands who wrote philosophy books, published a pamphlet defending my work. Shortly afterward, however, she went to India to open orphanages for the local children. Consequently there remained no one in this country to write a word in my defense.

In September of that year, I received a letter from Albert Burgh, whom I had met many years earlier in Franciscus van den Enden's house. When I was forced to leave Amsterdam following the rabbis' threats that they would ask the city authorities to banish me from the city, he was the man who provided me with accommodation in his father's house at Ouderkerke, in the vicinity of the Jewish cemetery.

"On leaving my country," wrote Albert in his letter, "I promised to write to you should anything worthy of note occur during my journey. Since such an occasion has now arisen, and one of the greatest importance, I am discharging my debt. I have to tell you that, through God's infinite mercy, I have been brought back to the Catholic Church and have been made a member thereof. The more I have admired you in the past for the insight and acuity of your mind, the more do I now moan and lament for you. For although you are a man of outstanding talent, with a mind on which God has bestowed splendid gifts, a lover of truth, and indeed a most eager one, yet you allow yourself to be entrapped and deceived by that most wretched and arrogant prince of evil spirits. For what does all your philosophy amount to except sheer illusion and chimera? Yet you entrust to it not only your peace of mind in this life but the eternal salvation of your soul."

There had long been rumors that the son of Conraad Burgh, one of the most affluent Dutchmen, walked barefoot and in rags in Padua, Venice, and Rome. He traveled between these cities on foot, as he had taken a vow of poverty and become a mendicant. The young man who once adored my interpretation of Descartes, who said he was not sure if he was a heretic or an atheist, but that he definitely was one or the other, now chose a third way, from which his parents could not turn him away. In his letter he promised to help me approach Christ, saying that after this I would be born again. He called my *Theological-Political Treatise* "an impious and diabolical book." He also wrote about the miracles of Jesus and the apostles, imploring me to avoid "the road of sin."

Albert's family asked me to answer his letter, hoping that my letter could make him return to the north. This is what I wrote to him: "Justice and charity are the one sure sign of the true Catholic faith, the true fruits of the Holy Spirit, and wherever these are found, there Christ really is, and where they are not, Christ is not. Had you been willing to meditate correctly on these things, you would not have ruined yourself, nor would you have brought bitter grief on your kinsfolk who now sorrowfully bewail your plight. I do not presume that I have found the best philosophy, but I know that what I understand is the true one. If you asked me how I know this, I would reply that I know this in the same way that you know that the three angles of a triangle are equal to two right angles. But you, who presume that you have at last found the best religion, or rather, the best people to whom you have pledged your credulity, how do you know that they are the best out of all those who have taught other religions, are teaching them now, or will teach them in the future? Have you examined all those religions, both ancient and modern, that are taught here and in India and throughout the whole world?"

One December morning, when opening the door for someone who had knocked, the servants in Conraad Burgh's house saw a man in rags, standing barefoot in the snow, and, thinking that he was a beggar, threw some bread to him, unaware that it was Albert Burgh. He had covered the distance from Rome to Amsterdam on foot. When I talked to him a week later, I was trying in vain to find a tiny bit of that Albert I once knew, to talk to that part of him and try to remove the shadow that obscured his mind. Reason could not be awakened in this man. A few days later he went back to Rome, where he died one evening when ripe apricots were falling from the trees in the monastery garden, having starved after many months of fasting.

A few months after seeing Albert, I met a young man who had previously tried to correspond with me, our correspondence ending after only a few letters. He came from Germany and his name was Leibniz. With his wig, he reminded me of Louis, the Sun King, but in his comportment he was very much like some of the court intellectuals I had met. Nevertheless, he looked to me to be more of a spy than a philosopher. His ludicrous figure and his conduct, which was indeed an odd blend of affability and arrogance—as well as his interest in philosophy, which he undoubtedly had a good command of—appeared to me to be a front concealing his intention to obtain important information for a German court. He showed great interest in my views on Cartesianism and in my metaphysics, commenting that it was full of paradoxes and yet praising it incessantly, while he was constantly coming up with questions regarding the Dutch Republic. This was the time when I had just started writing my *Political Treatise* (*Tractatus Politicus*), which was intended to start where the *Theological-Political Treatise* had stopped.

During the winter of 1676, my health, which had always been frail, began to deteriorate even further. One morning I told Hendrik van der Spyck that following my death, my desk and all my letters and writings should be sent to Rieuwertsz in Amsterdam. That winter I never left the house: I smoked my pipe, played with Hendrik and Margareta's children, and ate chicken soup on Sunday afternoons. I felt that death was around the corner, but I did not think about it, since a free man thinks least of all of death.

■ □ ■ □ ■

THREAD THREE

Freedom?

It is the end of 1676, you are lying on the bed with your face turned toward the wall. On the bedside table there is a half-burned candle. You are lying on your back, with your face still turned toward the wall. You are beginning to move your fingers, and their shadows make shapes on the wall. You are replaying your whole life in those shadows in a few brief moments: birth, writing, and death. You say that you feel that death is just around the corner and that you are not thinking about it, since a free man thinks least of all of death. Free from what?

Freedom and Affections

People live as slaves to their affections: desire, joy, sorrow, hatred, fear, hope. . . . What I call slavery is the human powerlessness to limit affections, since man, being subject to affections, is not his own master, but is subjugated to his destiny. He is often forced to choose the wrong path, even though he sees a better one. That man who is free of affections, possessing the knowledge of what is substance, attributes, and essence, is close to infinity and eternity. Hence a free man does not think of death.

The Portrait of the Philosopher as a Young Man, and the Portrait with the Weary Eyes

Let us go back to the end of 1676, or better still, let us go back to the beginning of 1677. You get up from your bed; you go to the window, looking through the square of the window where your life is now drawing to a close. It is winter, it is snowing, but you cannot see the snowflakes or the lanterns, you cannot even see the thick snow on the ground; your sight is blurred and everything you can see merges into a melting whiteness. Your portrait, painted when you were just over twenty, is hanging on the wall to the left of the window; on the right-hand side of the window is another portrait made just one year before your death. You are standing between the two portraits, framed by the window that you are slowly opening. On the left side, yourself at twenty. On the right side, yourself a year before your death. In the middle, your figure seen from the back, on the day of your death.

Let us have a look at the portrait on the left-hand side, Spinoza: an oil on canvas, showing you against a dark background. Your forehead is smooth and open, ready for what is to follow in your life, your eyebrows are curved like arches. Their beginnings near the top of your nose give an impression of decisiveness, and their slanted ends near your temples, of gentleness. Your lips in a tamed smile reflect an awareness of your intellectual superiority as well as a sensibility that, depending on the situation, can be upset by either sympathy or cynicism. Your eyes are not looking directly at the observer, as though you want to avoid any closeness. Nonetheless, there is a glow in your pupils, as though a piece of the moon is reflected there; by watching that glow more closely it is possible to catch your look. While looking at your pupils, however, there is a feeling that no one can enter into them unless that person becomes completely engulfed by them: there seems to be some kind of power emerging from your pupils that is itself penetrating and intercepts the scrutiny of others even before their gaze can slide over the glow of your pupils, preventing them from entering deeper into your eyes. I am looking at your portrait, Spinoza, the portrait of the philosopher as a young man, and I cannot tell whether or not it indeed represents a free man, a man free of affections, but I am confident that the young philosopher who is portrayed has decided to have no affections: he has firmly decided to fight them.

The other portrait, on the wall on the right-hand side of the window, a copper engraving made only twenty years or so after the first one, seems like a portrait of a completely different man, Spinoza. The sharpness of your nose, which suggests your readiness to face your opponents in the first portrait, is lost here. The arch of your eyebrows is almost imperceptibly broken—but broken nonetheless:

their beginning near the top of your nose no longer creates the impression of decisiveness, but of muddled withdrawal, and the slanted ends near your temples are no longer gentle, but dramatic. Your lips no longer reflect superiority but powerlessness. The pupils of your eyes possess no more of that glow like a piece of the moon being reflected. All this is not necessarily the result of the impact of time on you; it could also be the result of one of the disadvantages of the technique of copper engraving with which it is not easy to achieve the effect of a glow, unlike in an oil painting. If your eyes in the first portrait did not look directly at the observer, which indicated that you wished to avoid any closeness, your look here is one of total unattainability: it is now impossible to establish any closeness. An attempt to look into your pupils is once again unsuccessful: in the first portrait some kind of power seemed to emerge from your pupils, intercepting the scrutiny of others before their gaze could slip over the glow of your pupils, preventing them from entering deeper into your eyes; in this portrait your pupils have a certain blurry quality that then spreads all over your face, giving the impression of an oppressive sadness. And sorrow is an affection, isn't it, Spinoza? Moreover, the stamp of fatigue seems to be imprinted on your forehead; is this perhaps the exhaustion caused by your struggle against affections? A man who has been afraid of losing something all his life is now portrayed at the moment when he realizes that he has lost exactly what he has always feared losing the most. Life, Spinoza?

What you have told me so far is very interesting indeed, Spinoza. Your account has been balanced and witty, sometimes gentle and sometimes cynical, but this story seems to have been recounted by the young man with so much confidence in his eyes. However, I would like to hear the story of your life told once again, Spinoza. I would like to hear it told by the man with the weary eyes, the man who is far from being free, Spinoza, the man who is overwhelmed by affections, by that Spinoza who knew what despair and sorrow really meant.

■ □ ■ □ ■

THREAD FOUR

The Story of the Portrait with the Weary Eyes

Life, or what we call life, or, as it were, the beginning of dying, commenced at a definite point for me. Yes, I did exist even earlier, but it was not life: life begins with the first sign of death, and that sign was for me that definite point. Earlier, before that sign of death, there existed smells and tastes, there existed sounds, touches, forms, and colors, but none of these were interconnected. Everything looked like some kind of loop, a circle that presaged an endless process, an endless continuance, and not a line segment limited by a beginning and end.

Before the beginning of that segment, while I still existed within a circle, events were taking place witnessed by others; I, however, do not remember those events. I came into this world on 24 November 1632. Eight days after my birth I was given the name Bento, while people later also called me Baruch and Benedictus. All three names had the same meaning—"blessed"—although my life can perhaps be better described by my surname, which comes from the Portuguese word *espinosa*—meaning "thorn": a blessed thorn, or the blessed one among thorns, or blessing thorns, or throwing the blessed one onto thorns.

My mother's name was Hanna Deborah Nunes, and I never knew the name of the place where she was born. I knew for certain that she was born in Portugal twenty-four years before bringing me into the world. Somewhat earlier she had given birth to Isaac and Miriam.

In the evening, before going to sleep, I could hear my mother's warm voice singing psalms. Here are the first things I remember: my mother standing beside a window, the light coming in gives a silver glow to the contours of her figure, and she sings something I cannot understand. The next thing I remember is that I have learned to ask questions. I am asking her all kinds of questions: what is blood, what is a temple, what is Jerusalem, what are servants? And my mother has all the answers. I continue asking her: what is Babylon, what is a willow, what is a harp? Slowly, with that voice, a dream unfolds, and in that unmarked territory between dream and reality, I can hear the voice of my mother singing of the heathens who have invaded God's inheritance, defiled the holy temple, and laid Jerusalem in heaps. In my dream I am beginning to see how the heathens give the dead bodies of God's servants to be meat unto the fowls of the heaven, and the flesh of God's saints unto the beasts of the earth. I am dreaming how their blood is shed like water round about Jerusalem. Another evening her warm voice is singing about the rivers of Babylon, and once again the dream is rekindled inside me; I see men, women, and children sitting beside the rivers of Babylon crying and hanging their harps upon the willows. The warmth of her voice is slowly turning into a warmth created by some kind of sinking, by a total fall into something that is bottomless and is at the same time something that emerges, something that has no upper limits. My being seems to be turning into a dream that spreads continuously throughout a space with no boundaries.

The house with the orange paint peeling off is our house. There are carob trees in front of our house just as there are carob trees in front of all the other houses on our street. In spring and early summer I would wake up with the smell of carob trees: we, the children, slept in one of the attic rooms that the branches of a blossoming tree touched. Shortly before the carob trees finished flowering, my mother would come to our room, grab the branches, and pick the blossom. During the winter she made carob tea for all of us. In wintertime all of us slept in one of the ground-floor rooms where, close to the large red-canopied bed in which Mother and Father slept, there was a fireplace in front of which Father often stood. He would move his fingers in a magical way, their elongated shadows projecting onto the wall, symbolizing the fight between David and Goliath, or the suffering of Job, the righteous man. But what we wanted our father to show us most of all through this play of shadows was the Flood—its announcement by God, the building of the ark, the preservation of a pair of every animal species, the rain and the Flood itself, the search for land, the arrival on Ararat, and their final salvation. Father was engaged in the wood trade, among other things. I remember barges pulling tree trunks along the canals of Amsterdam, later carried to his shop, which bore the sign MICHAEL SPINOZA and which was situated in the street leading to the fish market. Some time later he abandoned this business, saying it was much easier for him to sell dried fruits, spices, and wine.

In the beginning, I preferred to stay in the attic room rather than in any other room in the house. I never went out to play with the other children in front of the houses: I just wanted to watch, to be an observer. During the night, if the barking of a dog or a nightmare woke me up (and such nightmares woke me up frequently in my childhood: I saw my mother and father moving away from me, running away from me, but when I caught up with them, they did not recognize me), I would quietly get up, not rousing Miriam, Isaac, and Rebecca from their sleep, open the window and look at the stars for a long time. I wanted them to be wormholes through which you could enter into another sky and from there, from the top of that other sky, see another city and another Bento wishing that through the window of his own room, he could reach a distant star. The thought of watching myself from above seemed both attractive and repugnant to me. I remember that the big mirror some people brought into our home one day, placing it near the fireplace, took me away from the window completely: instead of watching others, I began looking at myself. I stood bewildered in front of the mirror and became even more bewildered seeing my own bewilderment. I smiled and the smile would turn into laughter. As soon as my laughter subsided, I would touch my face as well as the face reflected in the smooth surface. Mother, lying on the bed even during the day, as she was often sick, watched me all the time and told me to go out and play with the other children. I refused; I stood in front of the mirror from morning to night until one day Mother told me that the mirror could charm me and swallow me up and that I might remain imprisoned on the other side forever. After her warning, I would glance at myself in the mirror for a fleeting moment as I passed by, to make sure that I really existed, but only for a very brief moment, lest I disappear into it.

I also remember the first time I visited the synagogue. It was situated in two connecting houses; in the first room there was a fountain where we washed our hands. I remember how the women separated themselves from us and went upstairs to sit in the balcony. I remember how I tried to see them when we entered the main room and how Father gave me a book and told me not to look upwards. Everyone wore over their caps white shawls that came down onto their shoulders, and everyone held books in their hands. Four men sat in the central section on a platform three feet higher than floor level where all of us were sitting. I later learned their names: Rabbi Mortera, Rabbi David Pardo, Rabbi Menasseh ben Israel, and Rabbi Isaac Aboab.

Coins were jingling, the scents of cinnamon, dried figs, dates, pepper, apples, and quinces mingled together, and the voice of the man who asked for Algerian pipes mixed with my whisper while I was reading something, sitting in the corner of my father's shop. When there were no customers, Father would sit close to me on the floor and say to me:

"You are going to be a rabbi. In two years you'll start going to school and one day you'll be a rabbi."

I turned the pages; I read them slowly but better than my brother Isaac who had been going to the Talmud Torah school every day and had taught me the alphabet.

"You are going to be a rabbi," repeated my father every day. One of the rabbis, Mortera, often came to our shop and bought mustard seeds, pepper, and tobacco, but never any sweets. Then I would move slowly around him, make circles around the rabbi who twisted his beard between his thumb and index finger, watching me. I just wanted to see how I would look one day when I became a rabbi.

All of a sudden the event that would interrupt my existence and mark the start of my life occurred. It began with the heavy breathing of Mother, her exhaustion evident, her whisper addressed to Father in the darkness of the night, when they thought that we, the children, were asleep, but I could hear them:

"I'm afraid of falling asleep. I'm afraid that if I fall asleep, I might forget to breathe."

THREAD FOUR

59
▾

At that moment all my dreams and my sleep lost their sweetness. I believed that if I tried not to fall asleep, I would help Mother not to fall asleep. I was afraid that if I did fall asleep she might also fall asleep and forget to breathe. The fear in me was so strong that I grabbed only brief periods of sleep during the day, when Mother was cooking or went to the market. When she returned, saying, "The carob trees have not flowered this year," I slowly opened my eyes, forgetting what I had just dreamed. Indeed, I kept on forgetting my dreams for virtually the rest of my life.

Soon Mother became too weak to go to the market or cook. Miriam took over most of Mother's domestic duties, as well as taking care of her: she made her tea and put cold and warm compresses on her forehead and chest. Within a few months I saw how a shadow of old age was spreading over Miriam's face. She was only nine at the time and, besides looking after the house and Mother, she had to take care of little Gabriel as well.

"The carob trees have not flowered this year," repeated Mother between two bouts of coughing, between two periods of dozing off on her thick pillow, between two morsels of bread soaked in milk. Soon she began to black out; even when she was awake she looked as if she were sleeping. Her pupils would not remain still, they seemed to vacillate, as if she was staring at a pendulum somewhere on the horizon, following its movements to and fro, again and again. Her powerlessness saddened me in a peculiar way, as if something pungent was poking me inside my chest, and I wanted to cry. It was a pain very much like when you hurt your knee after running and falling, or bite your tongue eating. Something, however, prevented me from crying and froze my voice. I was constantly hanging around the large red-canopied bed on which Mother was lying. I tried to smile, but my lips trembled. I am still puzzled how a six-year-old child like me could act in such a way, trying everything to cheer Mother up by whispering parts of the Torah in her ear or to make her angry by pinching her with my fingers or loudly stomping my feet on the floor close to where her head lay. But she remained motionless most of the time, breathing heavily—only her pupils were moving slightly, wavering to show that she no longer saw anything. One morning, following several days of silence and just after Miriam had given her some food, Mother opened her mouth and asked:

"Have the carob trees flowered?"

"It is too late for them to flower now. They've skipped this year. Snow has fallen already," said Miriam, looking out the window. When she turned to Mother, she saw that her pupils, the only thing that gave a sign of life to Mother's face, remained still and calm. "Mother," she cried and tried to bring her back to life, shaking her arm and sprinkling her face with water. "I'll go and fetch Father. Stay here!" she told me and ran out of the house.

Ever since I can remember, I have felt a need not to show my feelings in front of others, to hide them somewhere where no one will be able to see them, presenting a different mood, like the painter who puts a new layer of paint over the paint he hastily applied before, like the light of the stars that changes until it has reached this planet. While Miriam was still in the room, I watched everything that happened with great composure, almost indifference. But when she ran out of the room, I rushed to Mother, shivering, leaning my head on her bosom to be sure that she was still breathing. I believed that her life would be prolonged if I were there to hear her breathing. What I heard was a strange sound, something like a slow erosion, like a quiet and irreversible passing away. All of a sudden, something moved vigorously in her dying body. I could hear a sound mounting inside her, a sound that came from my mother's chest, a sound that instilled both fear and hope in me, a sound that was so strong and whose strength came from a mixture of the annunciation of death and the need to continue living. At that moment I believe I heard Mother whispering my name. I will never know whether I really heard those two syllables or I only wished I had heard them. I only know that I lifted my head and saw that the lips of Mother were blue and contorted, whereas her eyes were making an attempt to open. Her right hand made a barely perceptible movement, or at least it appeared to me to do so, a movement with which she tried to hold me and move me away at the same time. Then the strange sound in her chest grew very strong, turning into a cough that seemed to remain within rather than coming out, as she could barely open her blue lips. Her eyes opened slightly and her look, which was discernible under her dark eyelids, made me shudder from head to toe. I no longer recognized that look, it was completely alien to me, and the fear it caused inside me was even greater. It was obvious from Mother's pupils that I was also alien to her: she could not recognize me either. As her blue lips began to open due to her cough, I thought that the body lying on this bed was not the body of my mother, that the dark face, the mute lips, and the hostile look could not be hers. With the cough, blood came from the mouth of the body lying on the bed and flowed onto her chest. I was watching the blood, which was in sharp contrast to Mother's paleness, as if a piece of her soul had remained in the red fluid. I reached toward her chest, took a drop of blood between my thumb and index finger, and brought it close to my face, looking at the drop (the drop that seemed to pulsate between my thumb and index finger) as if it were the last thing in which I could see Mother. At that moment I felt something cold clenching my arm. But I did not look at where I felt the grip; I looked instead in the mirror. There my eyes met the dead eyes of Mother: they gazed into the mirror and from there they gazed into me. I remembered my mother's words, that the mirror could charm me and swallow me up. Hence I turned my eyes away from the mirror and looked at the drop of blood between my fingers, the last thing that bore witness to Mother's life. Then I looked at her, at her dead, half-open eyes, gazing into the mirror, and I became aware again of the cold grip on my arm. I looked at my wrist—the dead fingers of Mother were clenched there. Suddenly my fear turned into a scream, a scream that burst out loudly and penetratingly, an intense red scream that grew darker and darker, as my eyes moved along the triangle created by my mother's eyes, the fingers that powerfully clenched my wrist, and the drop of blood between my fingers. In the scream that grew darker and darker, there seemed to be something that was tearing apart deep inside me, moving away from me, but I was not aware what it was. Only the color of my scream, which was turning black as it began to die out, told me that I was losing something permanently and that the lifeless body that was gripping me so firmly was only a part of that loss.

By the time Miriam, Rebecca, and Father came running into the house, my scream had already died out. My voice now seemed so feeble that I could say neither yes nor no. Miriam and Rebecca began crying seeing Mother's body, and Father tried to remove the dead fingers of Mother from my wrist, shouting that I was turning blue, that I was breathing heavily, and that there was no blood in my hand.

He asked me to say something while he tried to release me from Mother's grip, but her fingers were clenched too tightly around my wrist. Just as I began to wish that I stay tied to her forever, that this remain an eternal bond—so that the loss would then only be partial—I saw Father spreading Mother's fingers enough for my hand to be pulled free. After that I ran to the corner of the room, curled up, and involuntarily fell asleep.

I did not go to Mother's funeral. I did not see her body put in a coffin, nor did I see her coffin put into a boat on the canal. I did not see her body being carried to the Jewish cemetery, and I did not see her buried in the ground. When I woke up two days later, my thumb and index finger were still tightly clenched together. I moved them apart and I saw a dry red speck. I put the speck in a handkerchief that I later always carried with me. It was this red speck that broke up the circle of my endless existence, turning my life into a line segment with a beginning and end. I noticed through the window that Father had cut down the carob trees in front of our house. Forgetful for a moment that Mother was dead, I thought that, since the trees were no longer there, she would never pick carob blossoms nor make us carob tea in winter again. After that, every winter, as early as the first days of November, I would begin breathing quickly and heavily, like when something is taken away from you, like when you have irreversibly lost something. Only a little bit of Mother remained in my memory: her hand giving me food, her figure reaching through the open window for the carob branches to pick their blossom, her foot stepping on and knocking over the little bowl of milk left at the door for the cat. I forgot how she used to sing sections of the Torah to me, I forgot how she used to explain the meaning of words to me, how she told me about the difference between a dream, imagination, and reality, I forgot how she told me that the mirror could charm me, I forgot how she was dying. All this did not occur consciously or deliberately; I forgot everything during those two days of sleep. Everything had been erased from my memory and all was lost until shortly before my death, the way you lose a heavy stone in a badly sewn pocket. After Mother died, I no longer had any dreams. I would begin remembering my dreams again only when my death was drawing near.

Miriam and Rebecca cried all the time that winter after Mother died. It was enough for them to open a drawer and see just one of

Mother's handkerchiefs (once a jar of rose preserves slipped from Rebecca's hands, breaking on the floor), and both would burst into tears. Sometimes I could not stay in the same room with them, since I had visions of Mother picking carob blossoms, giving me food, or knocking over the bowl of milk. I had to get away and run, crossing the bridges over the canals of Amsterdam. I came to despise tears: I would never again shed a tear in my life. In the evenings I was unable to fall asleep. I used to stay up late watching Father, who played chess against himself, or I invented stories and retold them to myself quietly so that no one would hear me. When I really wanted to sleep, I had to lie down and press the pillow firmly over my face so that the throb of my blood in my head sounded like the steps of sleep coming toward me.

I spent most of the time looking through the window or looking at myself in the mirror. I was no longer afraid that the mirror might charm me and that I would remain imprisoned there: I had forgotten what Mother had said to me. When there was no one in the large room on the ground floor, I stood in front of the smooth surface, looking at my face. I was no longer confused about there being another me there, nor did I laugh in front of the mirror anymore. I looked at the expression on my face—that quiet sorrow articulated in the trembling that became noticeable only after long and careful observation, a trembling that began imperceptibly near my chin, continued along the sides of my lips, mildly inclining downwards, and ending at my eyebrows. Under my eyebrows, the only undisturbed part of my face, were my eyes, but their calm, which stretched from the iris to the pupil and then seemed to continue deep inside them, further reinforced the impression of sorrow that was reflected in my face.

I developed a love of corners; they attracted me greatly. With unusual tenderness I would touch a book's corners. The corners of new rooms I went into fascinated me, arousing an inexplicable curiosity in me. I would go to one of the corners, and it seemed to me that there I was alone and that no one could hurt me or do me any harm. The next autumn after Mother's death, I started going to school, and while the other children jostled to sit in the front benches, I dragged myself to one of the classroom's corners. Later everybody noticed that wherever we went, I always wanted to be near the place where three lines met: in the synagogue's garden, in the schoolyard, everywhere. That is why, although I was recorded in the school books as Baruch, everyone called me Corner. When I looked through the window, I did not look through the window, but through the window's corners: I wanted to see that section of the external world framed by the window's corners. I no longer watched clouds moving across the sky, but clouds approaching one of the corners of the upper windowpane and then disappearing behind it. I no longer watched water flowing in the canal in front of our house; I watched how the canal was cut by the lower right-hand corner of the window.

My days in the Talmud Torah school were filled with a strange anguish. Everything was all right as long as the rabbis instructed us how to pray, as long as they explained the interpretations of the Torah and we translated texts. My anguish began at the instant the classes ended. I felt myself to be different from the rest of the children, and the children felt the same. They certainly could not see that I felt myself to be different, but they sensed I was different from them. In that difference, in my inability to talk to them as they talked to each other, they seemed to find a kind of inherent sin, something they chose to punish with contempt and hatred. Hence, immediately after the classes ended, at eleven o'clock sharp, I ran home, and came back to the school at two, only a minute before the afternoon classes began. Even during that one minute I felt extremely uncomfortable; I could feel them watching me, though I always stared at the corners of the table in front of me. At the same time, I could hear their voices very clearly, including the words of scorn they shouted at me, forcing me to make imperceptible movements toward the corner of the room. It was impossible to go any farther; I was virtually squeezed against the wall. The funniest thing of all for the children was when I sometimes took out my handkerchief, moved it between the fingers of one hand and the fingers of the other, and then put it back in my pocket again. Then they used to nudge each other, stare at me, and make fun of me, taking care not to be noticed by the teachers. One day, when the classes were over, some of the children from my form gathered in a group. Two of them took hold of me, a third took the handkerchief out of my pocket, and the rest started laughing loudly. Then they began to throw the handkerchief to each other, darting away from me as I tried to grab it from them. Finally, when they reached the bridge across the canal in front of the school, Joseph stretched out his hand, holding my handkerchief over the canal. I tried to snatch it, on the verge of tears from the pain of it, but he pushed me away, took one step farther, and opened his hand. I extended my arm as far as I could to catch the handkerchief, but it was too late. While I watched it falling into the canal, I thought that a part of Mother's soul, concentrated in that speck of blood on the white tissue, was merging with the water.

Every now and then I went to the Anatomy Theater, where the bodies of those sentenced to death were publicly dissected by surgeons a day after they had been hanged. A large crowd used to gather to watch the surgeons with their sharp knives cutting into pale skin, extricating veins and separating them from each other, reaching inside the body and pulling out the intestines and the heart, which appeared from the body's rib cage. These were the first bodies that filled me with excitement: someone's motionless arm, someone's closed eyes, someone's mouth rendered speechless forever, someone's hip and stomach. The dead bodies I had seen tormented me before going to sleep, and I also thought of them while I was reading Isaac the Blind's interpretations of the Torah. While I ate, instead of the piece of bread in my hand, I would see a dead finger that I had observed the previous day. I later wondered why the dead bodies held such a strong attraction for me. Why did they attract me so much? Why did they crawl into my thoughts more easily than living bodies? I knew it was because of my fear of losing something: you can lose nothing with a dead body; the dead body has already been lost, even before it might be desired or won. It was during those years that I changed from a child into a boy; dead bodies inhabited a large part of my imagination: however much I tried to fight it, I inadvertently imagined myself touching the cold crotches of corpses, inhaling the smell of death in their hair, passing my tongue over the most intimate parts of their bodies.

We never found out what Isaac's illness was. Father said that during the afternoon, while they were together in the shop, he suddenly saw his pale face. It was clear from his eyes that Isaac did not know where he was or who he was. Some people came and carried him home in their arms and put him on the canopied bed. He lay there with his mouth open, looking around, but recognizing no one. He had forgotten how to eat; we chewed the food for him and put it into his mouth, and he swallowed it. Doctors came to our house, but no one could tell us what his illness was. One day Isaac was no longer even able to swallow his food. It remained there already chewed up in his mouth. He did not even spit it out, and we had to take it out with our fingers. His skin grew more and more pale, and on the day that it became as translucent as the thinnest paper, Isaac died. At that moment something deep inside me trembled with the fear that I would never be able to drive away the scene I imagined, in which my body was entwined with that of my dead brother.

After the funeral, gathering up Isaac's clothes to throw them away, Father, without even looking at me, said:

"I have no more money to pay for your schooling. Besides, I need some help in the shop."

I said nothing. Father was a strange man: he wanted people to beg him. I was even stranger: I never wanted to beg. I knew that his greatest wish was that I become a rabbi. I knew that he would even borrow money to see me one day speaking in the middle of the synagogue. But I also knew another thing about him: aware that he was providing for someone, he wanted that person to demonstrate a passion for fulfilling what my father himself wished for and supported. His wish that I become a rabbi had developed over the years, growing ever more important, while I had always only listened to him, without uttering a word; as he told me about my future, I never ever said that I myself wanted to become a rabbi. He loved my silent acceptance of—or rather, my compliance with—his desire to make me a rabbi. But over the past year, I had said on two or three occasions: "When I become a rabbi. . . . " Now I am sure that at the precise moment when Father heard me saying that for the first time, the rabbinate was no longer an option for me. It is very likely that I would have become a rabbi had I not uttered the same words several times. I knew that the real reason for his decision to take me out of school was not because he could not afford it or that he needed someone to help him in the shop, because he continued to pay Rabbi Menasseh to tutor me privately, thereby showing everyone that he actually had the money. He terminated my schooling as a rabbi just to feel the pleasure of seeing my hopes turn to dust. I could only have given him greater pleasure if I had desperately begged him to allow me to continue my schooling, while he left me disappointed and helpless. It was as if he needed to feel like he was driving someone to death, even though he could have saved them with very little effort. Was this the result of his need to prove that he was someone of some importance in the world? Was his ambition to make decisions about other people's lives and thus add meaning to his own life? But I was not thinking of all that at that moment. I only knew that I had said nothing, though I am sure Father expected me to say something, to ask him something at least, if not to beg him or offer some resistance. From the very next day on I became a shopkeeper. I was seventeen and I never again mentioned anything about becoming a rabbi.

A few years later, Esther, my father's wife whom he married after Mother had died, fell seriously ill. Father spent most of the time at her bedside, cracking his fingers and praying to Yahweh to help her. One morning, while I was having breakfast, Father spoke to Esther who lay on the canopied bed:

"You'll live, you have to live. You mustn't die. . . . "

Esther, who had persistently said that she no longer wished to live, that she wanted to die rather than suffer, suddenly lifted her head and whispered:

"I must live. I have to live for at least another year. I want to live. . . . "

All of a sudden, the face of my father changed completely, over-whelmed by some kind of anger that seemed to be undermining his hopelessness. He told me that I did not need to go to the shop, since he planned to work there until noon.

Esther died that year. Five months later Father died too. The last thing he heard from me were my wishes for him to get well soon.

If there was anything I was grateful for about becoming a shop-keeper, it was my friendship with Franciscus van den Enden. He came one evening to the shop to buy dried figs and wine. Some-time later that evening I went with him to his home, where he and his friends talked about Paul of Venice, Giordano Bruno, and René Descartes. He liked unusual things. He himself looked unusual and behaved unusually, and probably I looked unusual to him too, baf-fling him by my behavior. We were very different. He was a short man approaching his sixtieth year. While he talked, as he raised and lowered his voice, he also raised and lowered his arms, and he filled the pauses between his sentences with a tapping sound that he made with his foot on the floor. While he was listening to someone else talking, he snapped his fingers or flicked them over his head as if he was arranging his hair, even though he was bald. He showed his confusion by beginning to scratch his earlobes. He did this with unusual nervousness if someone asked him a question or answered his question calmly and carefully, with no passion in his voice and no particular expression on his face—all this being part of his general demeanor. I, too, happened to ask questions and answer other people in the same way.

Later, as soon as the rumors spread around Amsterdam that I was to be excommunicated from the Jewish community, Franciscus told me that I could move into his home at any time, if I deemed it necessary. This was exactly what happened the evening after my brother had come from the synagogue and told me that the rabbis had proclaimed the *cherem*.

"I have to leave," I said. Gabriel did not say a word. "If I stay, it'll be your ruin too. If I leave, we can both be saved."

I got up from my chair and approached the large red bed. I touched its canopy, hid myself behind it, and then suddenly revealed my face with an apelike expression. Gabriel laughed and I laughed too. I stroked the red velvet. It was in this bed that Mother and Father had conceived Miriam, Isaac, me, Rebecca, and Gabriel, and it was in this bed that they died.

"I'll take the bed with me," I said. "I need nothing else. I'm taking only the bed."

I also thought that I wanted to take the window with the view through which the world started in my childhood. Then I ran upstairs to the attic. I opened the window and breathed in the cool smell of summer. I looked through the upper left-hand corner of the window; somewhere in the distance, in that cloudy night, there was a single star twinkling. It occurred to me that it was impossible to get there, and I felt somewhat sad about that. If only the stars were wormholes, then I could go to one of them, look through it and see a city, somewhere far away, on the other side, and there I would see someone else like myself gazing through another open window, asking himself what to do next. I left the room, leaving the window open; I went downstairs and stood for a while beside the canopied bed. Gabriel had fallen asleep sitting on the chair, with his head on the table. A candle was burning close to his face. I took the candle in my hands and went to the mirror. I had not really looked at myself in the mirror since my childhood. In the meantime I had used the mirror but only to see how I looked, whether my hair was well done or whether I should comb it a little more, whether my satin collar was in place, whether the dark color of my face was any paler because of my cold and the few days spent in bed. I could see that my eyebrows had curved into a regular arch form that gave the impression of decisiveness. My lips reflected superiority and cynicism in a tame smile, and if someone looked at my pupils, he would certainly know that he could not penetrate them unless he became completely engulfed by them. Some kind of power seemed to emanate from my pupils, a penetrating power. I tried to make a different facial expression, but this seemed impossible. I brought the candle back to the table and removed the few drops of wax that were drying on my fingers.

"Now I must leave," I said, waking Gabriel. He raised his head from the table, looking at me with sleepy eyes. "I'll send someone to take the bed one of these days," I said, putting my books in a bag.

It was a cool evening while I walked along the streets of Amsterdam with the bag of books on my back. I knew where to go. As soon as he had heard about my problems with the Jewish community, Franciscus van den Enden told me that his home was my home. Yet I did not go directly to his house. I needed to walk.

A man playing a street organ passed in front of our house. I went toward the Old Church, and from there to Jodenbreestraat: the homeless had already retired to their barrels, eating the leftovers from the food they had begged for. A woman, who looked at me with her left eye, her right one being closed due to a bruise, started running after me, shouting the price for one night. She lifted her dress up and pulled my sleeve. Two stout men started a fight in a gambling house after one of them had jumbled up the cards on the table. In the neighboring tavern, which smelled of smoked herring, people were standing up and singing with their glasses held high in their hands, while an old woman was sitting disconsolate at a corner table. Voices could be heard coming from the theater building—actors were rehearsing a play, while, in front of the theater, their children made paper boats from the pages of a book that showed corridors leading nowhere. They threw them down hoping that they would float on the canal water, but they sank. Then I walked along some narrow streets whose names I did not know, through lanes that smelled of freshly baked bread, of brandy, of roast pork and garlic, and also of urine and excrement. Hushed chatter or laughter could be heard in some of the streets. The sound of someone crying loudly came from an open window.

It was past midnight when I stopped in front of Franciscus's house. Lights were burning in two of the rooms: I assumed that Franciscus had spent the night in discussion with his friends. I knocked three times. When the door opened I saw Clara Maria's green eyes glowing in the dark.

"You should've come earlier," she said. "My father's been talking about the suffering of Isaac the Blind all evening."

The following day two porters carried the red-canopied bed to Franciscus's house.

I cannot remember how I became such a close friend of Clara Maria, how we had become as close as the knife and the bread. We had been friends even before my excommunication, before I had moved to Van den Enden's house. We felt close to each other ever since she gave me that first Latin lesson, and perhaps even earlier, when I used to meet her in the anteroom of their house, before and after the lessons Franciscus was giving me, when the only contact we had with one another was to say good morning and good-bye. Sometimes when her father's friends and I gathered in the house, she remained with us, but said nothing and only looked at us with the wild look you find in cats. When Franciscus would ask her to play something for us, she played the lute or harpsichord. After a while she began giving me lessons in Latin. She started her first class by telling me about the dream she had had the previous night. It was in this way that she started all of her lessons, and she ended them by asking me to recount one of my dreams in Latin. When I told her that I had no dreams at all, she said that I was either afraid of her and lied about not having any dreams or was afraid of myself and could not remember what I had dreamed. Perhaps I did have some odd fear of her, a fear that could not be explained by my definition of fear given later in my *Ethics*. It was a fear of becoming so close to another human being that I might finally merge with her, just as it was dangerous for the earth and the sun to come closer to each other, as this might lead to the burning of the entire living planet. And there certainly was a fear of myself, a fear that was basic and could easily be explained by facile definitions, a fear that also explained my fear of Clara Maria. On the other hand, I had no fear of her dreams—I remembered them. They always took place in a city that did not exist, but that, as she said, existed somewhere, a city established on the slopes of a mountain, in which life was lived according to the laws of childhood. In her dreams she always remained what she was—a child. Her dreams always ended in the same way: she walked over the roofs of the houses, unafraid of falling and yet always falling to the ground. Then she would get up and shake the dust off her clothes and see that a puddle of blood was all that remained of her fall.

Once she told me a dream about some people who greeted one another by touching each other's left ear with their hand, after which they made two circular movements around the ear. Then they would touch each other's left nostril, right nostril, mouth, and finally forehead. After that we always greeted each other in that way.

She also invented a special game: one of us had to quote a sentence from a book, and the other was supposed to guess who had written it. She usually went first: "*The entire cosmos consists of contradictions, but its harmony is based on disharmony.*"

"Baltasar Gracián," I replied. Now it was my turn: "*Never has so much thunder come from clear skies, never have so many dreadful comets shone over us.*"

"Virgil," said she and cited: "*Words do not fall into the void.*"

"Moses de Leon," I said, giving the name of the author of Zohar, and I quoted to her in turn: "*Wherever you go, whatever place you choose, the universe extends all over in an endless circle.*"

"Lucretius," she guessed, and then posed her quotation:
> *While he sought to quench his thirst,*
> *Another thirst grew in him, and as he drank,*
> *He was enchanted by the beautiful reflection he saw.*
> *He fell in love with an insubstantial hope,*
> *Mistaking a mere shadow for a real body.*

She always concluded the game with these lines from Ovid's *Metamorphoses*. We played the game quite often, but Clara Maria always, after a few rounds, recited the lines referring to Narcissus. When I mentioned to her that she incessantly repeated the same lines, she would only smile, spread her fingers, look at their shadow on the floor, and ask me a totally irrelevant question: Why is the sky above and not below? Or, Why does the day not begin in the evening and end in the morning?

Believe me, _____, I loved her questions. I know, this sounds silly to you, but I loved that meaningless exchange of words. Perhaps I did not like her questions as much as I liked her innocent and naive astonishment when faced with the miracle of existence. She would always begin asking her questions in a somewhat perplexed manner, but soon her face would light up, as if she was receiving the answer even before she had completed the question, as if she had seen the spectacle of an infinite answer that extended far beyond the explanation she had asked for, that clarified things that were so distant to us and about which we dared not even ask. At those moments her face was full of joy, the joy we feel when we have discovered something for the first time, when the world is new to us, when we are experiencing it in an innocent way with inquiring hands.

Yes, I know you believe me, _____, I know you believe me when I say that I, too, was overwhelmed with joy when I entered her room, when she was translating aloud parts of *The Anatomy of Melancholy* for herself, or was playing the harpsichord. She would then turn around, look at me and say:

"Bento"—she always called me Bento, never Baruch, never Benedictus—"listen to these words, '*I can thus discover antecedents to my current distress in a loss, death, or grief over someone or something that I once loved.*' Do these words know that I am reading them at this very moment?" and she closed the book and put it aside. If she was playing an instrument, having played the last note, she would ask, "Do these sounds know that I am giving life to them?"

"Probably they do not know it themselves, but that which embraces them in itself knows."

"God?"

"You can call it God. Or Creative Nature. Or substance. Substance is that which is in itself and is conceived through itself."

"So the words I'm reading, the notes I'm playing, are not in themselves and cannot be conceived through themselves?"

"The sounds themselves, the words themselves are mere modifications of the infinite substance; that substance permeates both the words and sounds. So a part of them, that part which is the very idea of themselves, and is thus a part of substance, conceives their essence."

"What is the difference between essence and substance?"

"The essence of substance is expressed only through the attributes and in them."

"What are attributes?"

"Substance itself consists of an infinity of attributes through which it expresses its essence, and it is from these attributes that eternal and infinite modes are created. Of this infinity of attributes we can comprehend only two: Thought and Extension. These two attributes are in constant association. An infinity of modes are derived from each attribute, which are in fact modifications, or states, of substance. Modes are individual things through which substance is manifested and are derived from attributes, just as attributes are derived from substance. Everything that is derived directly from substance and attributes is again infinite and eternal—as are the infinite and eternal modes: the mode of motion and rest comes from the attribute of Extension, the mode of the infinite intellect comes from the attribute of Thought, and the appearance of the entire universe comes from the encounter of these two attributes. Seen through the attribute of Extension, the modes are bodies; seen through the attribute of Thought, the modes are ideas. The infinite and eternal mode of motion and rest is the sum total of all bodies, which are finite modes, and contains in itself all motion and rest. The infinite and eternal mode identified as the infinite intellect contains in itself all individual ideas. The infinite and eternal mode identified as the appearance of the entire universe contains in itself the wholeness of the world and is the sum total of the laws of the relationship between transient and finite modes. So we now come to the transient and finite modes, whose number is countless, as opposed to eternal and infinite modes, of which there are only three; the number of transient and finite modes is equal to the number of transient and finite bodies in the world. In both modes, essence does not coincide with existence. This is how the fall from perfection to imperfection takes place: attributes come from substance, eternal and infinite modes come from attributes, the countless transient and finite modes—bodies—come from eternal and infinite modes. Perfection is Creative Nature (*Natura naturans*), and that is substance and attributes; imperfection is Created Nature (*Natura naturata*), and that is modes. Creative Nature can be conceived only through itself; Created Nature can be conceived only through substance."

"I think I haven't quite understood how the attributes determine whether something will be an idea or a body. . . . "

"This is because an attribute is like a viewpoint. You're always the same, but if I look at you from here, I can see only the right side of your face, I can see your right eye, which has a questioning look, and your hair at the top of your forehead. If I go to the other side"—and I repositioned myself—"I can see the left side of your face, I can see your left eye, which offers the answer, and your hair, which is falling over your face. I can also see your fingers playing with the book's pages, or the movement of your bosom breathing in and out. I can see your nostrils or the place where your neck and collarbone meet, or see the place where your back ends and your neck commences. Then I am just an attribute, I am only a point that observes you, while you're always the same, you're always Clara Maria, regardless of what part of you I choose to observe. In the same way, the modes of various attributes are always one and the same modification, and they differ only in their viewpoints. Hence both the body and the soul are the same thing: one seen through the attribute of Extension, and the other through the attribute of Thought."

"But I still cannot quite understand the connection between all these things, between substance, attributes, and essence, between eternal and infinite modes, and between transient and finite modes," she said, leaning on the harpsichord.

"Let us imagine that substance is light, but not light coming from a specific body, such as the sun, a star, or a candle. Let us imagine that this light representing substance has created itself, that it is self-permeating, infinite, and eternal. Then we can imagine attributes as an infinity of prisms, prisms that have been created by the light/substance itself; these prisms/attributes, unlike those we know, are infinite and eternal. So, the only similarity between these prisms/attributes and the prisms of our world is their power to refract light. Light/substance expresses its essence passing through prisms/attributes while it is being refracted there. Hence substance expresses itself, attributes express, and essence is expressed. It is precisely after this refraction of light through attributes that its modifications are created. Three eternal and infinite modes are created first:

THREAD FOUR

we can imagine them as primary flashes of light, but not flashes as we know them, not flashes that are brief and limited in space, but flashes of light that are infinite and eternal. The playful colors of refracted light are then created from them—these are finite and transient modes. In other words: light passes through prisms, primary flashes of light are created, and in the end different colors are formed." I looked at her. "Is it any clearer to you now?"

She just smiled and struck a few notes on the harpsichord.

"Nonetheless," she said, "tones can nonetheless be conceived through themselves. The same goes for words." After playing several bars, she looked at me and added: "Besides, the playful colors of light are sometimes more beautiful than light itself, however short-lived they may be. Or perhaps precisely because of that."

After I moved to Van den Enden's house, following my excommunication from the Jewish community, I slept in the room next to hers.

The night I arrived, after all the people who had come to talk to her father left the house, Clara Maria asked me, while making my bed up, "What does Baltasar Gracián mean when he says that all things in this world should be looked at from the opposite angle if we want to truly understand them?" I do not remember what my answer was. I only remember that I could not get a wink of sleep that night, thinking that she was sleeping in the next room.

A month before I moved into their home, Clara Maria's mother had died. Clara Maria never showed any sorrow, no one had ever seen her crying, but she started going out more often and would not return home for a long time, sometimes not before dusk. One November afternoon I joined her. We came to the outskirts of the city and then continued to walk in the fields.

"Who am I?" asked Clara Maria slowly. I looked at her perplexed. "Clara Maria," she said. Then she repeated this at a faster and faster pace: "Who am I? Clara Maria. Who am I? Clara Maria. Who am I? Clara Maria." She began to walk faster just as she was speaking faster. After a while, exhausted from speaking and walking, she fell to the ground, but went on asking herself the same question and replying to it. When the speed of her speech became so fast that her tongue began twisting around in her mouth and her face became contorted, she repeated her questions and answers just a few more times and then stopped uttering any sounds. I was looking at her all the time.

After that she explained to me that she experienced a wonderful moment when she forgot not only what her name was but also what the question was, and not only that but also who had asked the question in the first place. She said that during those moments she actually felt who she really was.

"Will you try it yourself?" she said.

I opened my mouth, but I could say nothing. A little later, when I tried it once more, the same thing happened again.

I started running. I thought running might help me ask myself who I was. She was running after me. The sound of her steps seemed to pursue me, and the feeling that someone was running behind me made it even more difficult to ask as simple a question as that.

"Who am I?" I finally managed to utter and I stopped.

Clara Maria caught up with me. She stood before me and looked into my eyes. I was watching her intently, with the gaze of someone who had forgotten everything, including who he was.

"Who are you?" she asked me.

I remained silent for a while and then said.

"Bento? . . . Baruch? . . . Benedictus? . . . I don't know."

I turned and started running. Something strong buzzed in my ears and I could no longer hear her steps, but I knew she was running after me. I fell to the ground. She caught up with me. She helped me get up. Then she put her fingers on my cheeks.

"Feel how cold they are," she said.

I wished that it all could last forever. I wished that any of those moments could be transformed into an infinite continuance and that all of them would carry on at the same time. I wished that the lifting of her fingers lasted endlessly, at the same time as the opening of her mouth. I wished that the utterance of her words, *Feel how cold they are,* and her cold touch on my cheeks continued beyond all measurable time and existence. Eternity attracted me desperately, or rather, I was infinitely afraid of endings.

And yet everything had to end. It had to end with my departure from Van den Enden's home. I was compelled to leave Amsterdam having spent the last two days in Franciscus's house alone with Clara Maria, while he and his two younger daughters were away on a visit to their cousins in Antwerp.

THREAD FOUR

■ □ ■ □ ■

THREAD FIVE

Escape

It is nighttime and the moonlight falls across your hand. This is your last night in Van den Enden's home. Only the sound of the lute can be heard from the room next to yours. You close your eyes: Clara Maria appears in the dark of your closed eyes—she sits beside the open window and her fingers are running over the strings of her instrument. Everything moves in a barely perceptible manner, in some peculiar state between trembling and throbbing: Clara Maria's fingers and her nostrils, the lute's strings, and the dark curtains beside the open window, which are fluttering in the breeze. The air in the room is vibrating with the sound of music, and because of the motion of the clouds in the night sky, the moon itself seems to be moving. You are running the fingers of your left hand over your open right palm. You do this slowly, as slowly as the music Clara Maria is playing. The music stops, and all of a sudden you lose Clara Maria's face in your closed eyes. You open your eyes and go toward the door. You lift your hand to open the door, but you stop. Are you hesitant, Spinoza?

■ □ ■ □ ■

I imagined myself approaching her, while her eyes tried to avoid my pupils as she was breathing and gasping for air a little. I imagined myself slowly undressing her while she paused between breathing in and breathing out, between breathing out and breathing in, as if she was carrying the air to some unknown place. I imagined myself undressing her quickly and then us lying close to each other; I could feel the warmth of her thighs. I imagined myself slowly going into her, and then my fantasy suddenly came to an end. My hand was making a final movement on my penis as I ejected my semen.

I was lying on the canopied bed, feeling the wet semen on my belly. I heard steps and then several knocks at the door. The door opened.

"I can't sleep," she said. "It's a full moon."

I moved the blanket aside and sat up in the bed.

"You can't sleep when the moon is full either, can you?"

"I can't sleep at all," I said, rubbing my eyes.

"I'd like to read you something," she said, opening *The Anatomy of Melancholy* by Robert Burton. "Can I light a candle?"

"Please don't," I said, afraid that she might notice the wet substance on my belly. "The moonlight is enough."

She went to the window and began translating from the book for me: "*For those who are racked by melancholy, writing about it would have meaning only if writing sprang out of that very melancholy. I am trying to address an abyss of sorrow, a noncommunicable grief that at times, and often for a long time, lays claim upon us to the extent of having us lose all interest in words, action, and even life itself.*"

She closed the book, leaving it beside the window. She sat close to me on the bed. I heard her sniffing.

"There is a strange smell in here."

"Yes, that's right," I said, believing that she had never before smelled semen and that she could not tell what the smell was.

She moved her head closer to me and began sniffing.

"It is you who smells like this. A strange smell indeed."

She moved her head away, placed her legs on the bed, and moved closer to the wall, leaning on it.

"How much can you learn about something new through smell?"

"You can learn nothing through smell. For you can learn nothing through sensory experience. We can learn nothing through our senses, for as long as we try to grasp the essence of something through our senses, we only perceive the effect of that something on our body. This is not true knowledge—it is only the perception of an imprint, a mere trace of the physical upon the physical."

"What if I touch you?" And she put her finger on my back. "Is this, too, just an imprint, a mere trace?"

"Yes," I said. "It is only through our reason that we can gain an adequate idea about things."

"So not even through this movement, not even through running my finger over your back can I know anything about you?" she asked me, while her finger was moving down my back with the tenderness of a falling leaf.

"I've already told you: you can learn nothing of truth through sensory experience. The perception received through our senses is never the essence of something; it is only its appearance."

"So any attempt to learn about something through sensory experience must end in absolute ignorance."

"No. Absolute ignorance means not knowing anything. If we try to learn about things through sensory experience, it is a situation where knowledge is lacking, and a lack of knowledge is inaccurate knowledge: knowledge composed of inadequate ideas. That knowledge is inadequate in two ways: there is a lack of knowledge about ourselves and a lack of knowledge about the object that creates affection in us." I looked at her finger. "So we will know neither ourselves nor the one we touch."

"How can we know ourselves and the one we touch?" she asked.

"We can understand things in two ways: we can either understand them in correlation to a specific time and place or understand them as being part of God and originating from the determination of divine nature. It is only using the second method that we can truly understand things: then we can understand them from the perspective of eternity, as their ideas contain the eternal and infinite divine essence within themselves. Our soul is itself an idea; it is but a modification of God in the attribute of Thought, just as our body is the modification of God in the attribute of Extension. The goal is to start from the soul and the body, which are merely modifications, and arrive, through the attributes, to the idea about them in God, to pure essence."

She sighed and asked:

"But what if . . . what if my finger can think more than my mind? What if the idea of your own being is not somewhere outside you? What if your essence is not in God, but is actually here, under my finger, on this very spot? And what if this trace, this imprint, this touch, embraces you in itself, all your joys, yearnings, and despair, and at the same time embraces me and all my yearnings and despair? What if this place, where my skin and your skin meet each other, is the place where our beings meet? What if the encounter of our very essence is precisely here, not somewhere outside ourselves, not elsewhere?"

I did not say anything, and she went on:

"What if there is neither essence nor substance, what if there are no attributes, and what if these are only your ideas? What if God is only an idea in your mind and you are not an idea in God? What if only these bodies exist and nothing else exists apart from them? How would you learn about things then?" She removed the finger from me and put it on her forehead. "Then I'll learn about myself through touch," she said and, laughing, began touching her belly, breasts, and shoulders. These brief touches and her giggle reminded me of her age: I remembered that she was only fifteen. "I'll learn about myself through smell," she said, pulled a few locks of hair to her nose, and then sniffed her fingers. Then she took her feet in her hands, put them close to her nose, and smelled them. "I'll learn about myself through sound," she said, producing some strange sounds with her lips, like the blowing of a mournful wind late at night, like the embers of a dying fire, like the crunching of brittle soil under firm footsteps, like a drop of water being lost in an endless sea. She seemed to be listening to all these sounds, but then she paused and added: "No, not through these alien sounds, but through the sounds of my body will I learn about myself." She put the pulse in her wrist to her ear. "It beats like the heart," she said, listening to it with her eyes closed. "I'll learn about myself through sight," and she opened her eyes and looked at herself bathed in the milky moonlight. She looked at the palms of her hands and her ankles; she turned her head and tried to look at her back over her shoulder. "I'll learn about myself through taste," she said and licked the ends of her fingers, she sucked the soft flesh on the inside of her elbow, she bit the ends of her hair. Then she stopped giggling. She rearranged her hair, the last thing through which she wanted to learn about herself. "Have you ever tried to learn something about me?"

"Yes, I have," I said.

"As an idea in God?" she asked, caressing her lower lip.

"Yes, as an idea in God," I repeated.

THREAD FIVE

"What is your adequate idea about me then?" she asked, smiling.

I closed my eyes and sighed. She knew I would not answer her question, or perhaps she did not even need an answer, and hurriedly asked me another:

"But what if we obtain all our true ideas through smell and touch, what if adequate ideas come from tasting and seeing? What if they are the result of sensory experience? What if it is only through physical traces, through physical imprints, through such reflections of the physical, that you can learn about others? Would you then look for my essence through touching me, smelling me, watching me, tasting parts of my skin, of my hair, of my urine, listening to me?" She did not wait for an answer, but jumped up from the bed and hastened toward the door.

I watched her leaving my room. Only the smell of her body remained with me. As I had the sensation of her smell keeping in rhythm with the throbbing of my penis, I tried to convince myself that passion was an affection and that through affections man would only enslave his own soul. But my efforts were in vain: all I could see with my eyes closed was her body.

I got out of bed and left my room. Walking in the hall I noticed that the door of the library and music room was open. There was Clara Maria leaning on the harpsichord, crying. I came up to her and put my hand on her head.

"Why are you crying?"

"For Echo the nymph," she said and began reciting:

Only her voice and her bones were left.
Till finally her voice alone remained,
For her bones, they say, were turned to stone.
Since then, she hides in the woods, and,
Though never seen on the mountains, is heard there by all,
For her voice is the only part of her that still lives.

She wiped her tears. "It's time for me to go to bed," she said and went to her room.

I took Ovid's *Metamorphoses* from the library and read the section on Narcissus and Echo. At the time I could not understand why Clara Maria cried. Now I know.

The following day I left for Ouderkerke. I stayed for a year and a half in this village, which was near the cemetery where the Jews of

Amsterdam buried their kin. I then moved to Rijnsburg. It was there that I once again felt my helplessness in the face of affections.

As I now recall all this, everything seems so wonderful to me, like a tongue twister whose words have no meaning and yet can mean everything, like leaving prints of your lips on a steamy windowpane. At the time, however, I was not very happy with Johannes Casearius's inattentiveness, with his inability to conform to ideas and follow them, and with his almost somnambulistic fascination with space. He appeared one morning at my house in Rijnsburg. "Good morning," he greeted me. "My name is Johannes Casearius," he introduced himself, "and I've been told that you are Benedictus Spinoza." He explained that he was studying philosophy at the University of Leiden and asked me to give him lessons on the teachings of Descartes. "I'll come here every Saturday and go back to Leiden on Sunday evening," he said, adding that he would pay for the lessons on a regular basis. I supported myself by, among other things, tutoring in philosophy and mathematics, and I had six or seven students at the time. Taking Johannes as another student should not have been a problem, but there was something coarse about him, a kind of simplicity that bordered on crudeness. In his presence you felt as if you were holding a piece of glass that was not smooth enough, while at the same time this glass seemed to refract the rays of light in the most wonderful way, as if its roughest part contributed to a dazzling play of light that, passing through it, created the most beautiful colors and figures on the white wall of existence.

Indeed, his inability to comprehend ideas dismayed me. I spoke to him about the teachings of Descartes on the divine action according to one's own free will, and he made the shapes of circles, triangles, and squares with his eyes. I asked him what he was looking at, and he said that he was trying to picture God with his eyes: for what was the purpose of a knowledge of God if you could not picture him with your eyes, if you could not see him? He seemed quite hopeless as a student to me, because of his inability to understand the entirety of the philosopher's teachings. He would choose a single word and lose himself completely in that word, in a world of imagined forms. Now I believe that he explored things as they should be explored: his aim was to experience things that I only began to think about.

"I'd like to stay and live in this house," he said to me one Saturday morning, immediately after his arrival from Leiden. I was not sure whether to agree or not: I noticed his bags in which he had probably put everything he needed until early spring.

One day, while we were walking through the snow and I spoke to him about the separateness of Extension and Thought according to Descartes, he said:

"You know what? I have a feeling that right there where you're standing at this precise moment in the snow, there's a flower."

I stepped aside, and he cleared the snow that I had trodden on and compacted. And indeed, on the ground beneath the snow, there lay a flattened flower.

When we dined he watched me with a peculiar ferocity and tenderness at the same time, strengthening the hesitation in my soul, reinforcing the simultaneous repulsion and attraction I felt for him by bringing them closer together, making them rub against each other, emitting sparks. I was perplexed and could not fathom my hesitation. I watched him and stopped eating several times. He burst out laughing, choking on his food. Pieces of chewed food spurted out of his mouth going all over the place. He explained to me that I had been staring at him in such an odd way, it was as though I was trying to choose a horse to buy.

"Have you ever bought a horse?" he asked me, collecting the pieces of food scattered all over the table and putting them back into his mouth.

"No," I replied.

"Would I be right in saying that you are not a rider?" he said.

"No, I am not a rider. How did you guess?"

"By the way you walk."

"How do I walk?" I asked him.

"Like a man who doesn't know how to ride a horse," he said and began laughing again. "I'd like to teach you to ride," he continued. "If it weren't for this winter weather, I'd have started today. We could try it today, but it'd be too dangerous for you."

"Where did you learn to ride?"

"I was born in the country," he said. He turned the chair around and sat straddling it, as if he was riding it. "I'm better at riding and reaping than at reading books. After my father died, my mother couldn't support all of us seven children. She gave me up for adoption to a family in Leiden when I was ten. It was only then that I began to learn how to read and write."

The next day, while I spoke to him about my disagreement with Descartes' teaching concerning the absolute freedom of the human spirit, Johannes interrupted me, saying: "I dreamed about you last night. We were riding horses together."

■ □ ■ □ ■

Did you dream about him, too? Did you see him in the dreams you could not remember, those that escaped your memory as soon as you opened your eyes?

The Dead Body's Fear

I imagined him. I imagined him approaching, as peasants approach horses, with both brutality and tenderness. I imagined him coming near me with his breath and touch, while my soul, the soul of the one who imagined all this, was hesitant. My soul was struggling between pleasure and disgust, but the body of my other I, of the imagined I, was not hesitant at all. That body accepted the game and returned the touches, caresses, blows, and sighs. While imagining all this, I sensed my hand making the last act of stimulation on my penis, ejecting semen and spilling it on my belly.

The door opened.

"I can't sleep."

"You can't sleep when the moon is full, can you?" I asked him and made a short movement with my hand to remove the blanket from my body. Then it occurred to me that he could smell semen.

"I didn't notice it was a full moon. I can never sleep after I've had wine. But you can't sleep when the moon is full, is that right?"

"I can't sleep at all," I said and sat up in the bed, wrapping my body in the blanket.

"You're not angry that I came to your room without knocking at this time of the night, are you?"

"No," I replied.

He sat on the chair across from the bed.

"Can I stay a little while in your room?"

"Yes, of course," I said.

"I was about to ask you," he said and then paused, breathing the air in deeply. He had smelled semen. "Since I've come here you are always telling me about ideas, intuition, knowledge. But you've never told me anything about tangible things."

"According to Descartes . . . "

"No, not according to Descartes. Tell me something about tangible things according to your philosophy."

"First of all, you have to understand that there is a difference between matter and form."

"Isn't matter what form is created from?"

"Exactly. That is why matter is not the same as form; it precedes form. Form is a pure negation, and negation is not something positive. It is quite clear that matter, which is one of the three eternal and infinite modes of substance, taken in its entirety and being undefined, can have no form, since form belongs only to limited, finite bodies. If someone says, 'I understand a certain form,' he indicates that he understands something that is defined and exists within certain limits. This definition does not refer to the very essence of something, but rather expresses its nonessence. Form, accordingly, is merely a definition, and definition is a negation. Hence form can only be a negation."

"This means that bodies are a negation, doesn't it?"

"Taken in itself, separately from the soul, the body is a negation. The essence of man consists of certain modes of the divine attributes: of the mode of Thought, without doubt; hence the human soul is part of the infinite divine mind. The object of the idea constituting the human soul is the body, which is a specific mode of Extension. The soul and the body are one and the same individual entity, which is sometimes understood under the attribute of Thought and sometimes under the attribute of Extension. The human soul is the very idea of the human body in God."

"But isn't the human body an idea in God as well?"

"No. I've already told you: the human soul is the very idea of the human body in God."

"So the body doesn't exist in God? Is that why it is a negation?"

"I would like to think about that," I said. "I cannot answer your question right away. At this moment I can only tell you that a negation is something that limits or is limited. The body is a negation, because it is not infinite."

"So I should wish that my body be infinite so that it wouldn't be a negation, shouldn't I?"

I laughed.

"I think you tend to oversimplify things."

"So what should I do if I don't want my body to be a negation?"

"The body is a form, the body cannot turn into formlessness. Losing its form, the body ceases to be a body. It thus follows that the body is a negation as long as it exists. It is impossible for the body to be infinite."

"So how can we attain infinity?"

"With our reason."

I spoke to him about the three types of knowledge. He could not understand anything. Then I told him:

"My reason gives me enjoyment. I enjoy infinity."

"What about finite, limited bodies?"

"No. I only enjoy infinity."

"And you never want your body to give you enjoyment?"

"No," I said. "The body is not infinite."

"But let us imagine that it were. Let us imagine that bodies were infinite. Even if they were not, why should we not take the opportunity to enjoy the body and the enjoyment it brings?"

"I've already told you: I only enjoy infinity."

"But if the body and the soul form the same individual entity and if a part of the soul is infinite, then the body, too, must possess an infinite part."

"Infinite is that part of the soul that is dedicated to the knowledge of infinite things. The body cannot acquire such knowledge—the body is limited."

"But why shouldn't you examine the limitations of the body before coming to know the infinity of the soul?"

I did not know what to say.

"Why would you only have indications of those limitations? Lie down. Now think for a moment that you are dead, that you no longer exist. I really can't tell you what part of you should no longer exist and what part you should have to think no longer exists: whether it is your body or your reason. If you want to experience limitation, then forget about reason: experience the body and nothing else. Think that you only have that dead body and that it is reason that has disappeared. But if you want to experience infinity, then forget you have a body, think that the body, once it is dead, is no longer there and that reason is what continues to exist. Both things are possible if you think that you are dead. The most important thing is to imagine that you are dead."

My body shuddered from a convulsion that passed through it. I did not know why, but at the time I believed that a free man thought least of all of death, and I did not particularly look for the reason for my intense embarrassment due to Johannes's instructing me to imagine myself dead. Now I know that the irredeemable and forcibly forgotten loss of my mother when I was a child has always haunted me. Now I know that while I was lying on the canopied bed and Johannes told me to imagine myself dead, somewhere deep in my mind, in a place I could not access at that time, the memories of Mother's dead body lying on the red-canopied bed were stirred. At the time I believed that anything that might happen between me and Johannes would only arouse ever new affections in me, drawing me away from true knowledge. For this reason, I got out of bed and told him: "It's time for you to go to your room. I have to sleep."

"I'd like to stay with you tonight," he said and put his hand on my shoulder, drawing me closer to him and the bed. I felt I was breathing in the air he was breathing out. Our eyes met, I tried to avoid them, but ended up looking at him again.

"I have to sleep," I said, afraid of what might happen if we stayed together in the same room any longer.

After he had closed the door, I thought of what might have happened if I had not told him to leave the room. "What then?" I wondered. I imagined that he would stay and live with me in Rijnsburg. "What then?" The question turned my imaginings into nonsense. Each *What then?* led me to a desolate end, like a road that ends in the middle of a field or at the edge of an abyss, like a sentence whose last words are "and yet," wiping out the meaning of what has been said earlier, while no new meaning is offered. I wished he were dead. I was lying with my eyes closed, with my hands over my eyes. The moonlight disturbed me. I imagined him dead. I imagined him lying somewhere, forgotten in the middle of a field and disintegrating. I imagined him lying there mute and hoped that the question *What then?* would never come back to haunt me. Indeed, that question was not there while I imagined Johannes dead, but the yearning for dead bodies reemerged, the yearning that I had felt a long time before when I was still a child, observing the dissections in the Anatomy Theater. I imagined Johannes lying dead in a field, and I struggled not to go there, I fought against my urge to run my fingers over his cold skin, I fought against my desire to put my lips on his discolored mouth, I fought against my desire to pass my penis over his stiff body.

The next morning, while we were having breakfast, the liveliness of his movements bothered me, his effervescence caused me pain. I watched him while he put food into his mouth, trying to catch a glimpse of me between two sips of milk. It seemed to me that his life was taking something away from my existence. At the time I believed that passion would interfere with the creation of my adequate ideas. At the time I believed that affections would interfere with dedicating myself fully to the intellectual love of God. Now I know, however, that it was nothing more than a fear of the end. The thought that everything was about to end sooner or later made me put an end to anything before it had even begun.

"Johannes," I said and paused, noticing that I pronounced his name for the first time in my life. He looked at me. "You should leave. I can no longer give you any lessons."

He did not ask for an explanation. He left the same day at noon. As he was leaving, he found a dead bird on the road. He bent down, stretched out his fingers to touch it, but stopped, shook his hand, as though he wanted to free himself of something, and continued down the road.

From time to time, on some of the envelopes of the letters I received, I recognized his handwriting: "Professor Benedictus Spinoza." I never opened those letters. I put them away, like a wine that would not be too agreeable to drink after you've had beans and peppers. I kept them beside the window through which I could see the meadow where Johannes had once found a flower that I had trodden on under the snow. It was in such a meadow that I had wished to see him dead—motionless and mute—so that his existence would cause me no further pain. Upon leaving Rijnsburg, I left all of his letters, inadvertently or deliberately, there, beside the window.

THREAD FIVE

A Letter and Three Pressed Flowers

Dear Mr. Spinoza,

I am not sure if you still remember me, but I have never forgotten you. I have occasionally sent you letters, at your address in Rijnsburg. A friend of yours, Mariet Meester, has recently visited me and told me that you no longer lived there, that you had moved out of the house, and that you now live in The Hague. She has also given me the address to which I am now writing to you. Although a long time has elapsed since then, I believe you must remember me. We spent several months together in Rijnsburg, and you tutored me in Cartesian philosophy. I have been distanced from philosophy for a long time now, as I indeed have been from our northern country, but I often think of you. This may come as a surprise to you, but I have always had a strange feeling for you, something that is very difficult for me to explain, and I always tend to explain things in the wrong way, as you very well know. Anyway, I think that you were aware of my feelings, and perhaps the same kinds of feelings were also aroused in you too. I am so confused, especially knowing that you will definitely receive this letter; I do not know how to explain everything, though I have nothing in particular to write to you. I have already written you that I have been very far from both philosophy and the Netherlands for a long time, and yet I have not told you where I am and what my current preoccupations are. You should know that since you told me that you would no longer tutor me, I quit my philosophy studies altogether. I became a priest, but I did not stay in the Reformed Church for long either. As a missionary priest, I went to the Dutch colony on the southwestern coast of India, to Malabar. Dear Mr. Spinoza, it is so sunny and warm here that I often think of you, of your frail health, and of how agreeable it would be for you if you lived here. You see, I have again strayed from what I wanted to tell you. As a matter of fact, I am so confused that I have probably forgotten what I really wanted to tell you. Perhaps I should start writing this letter from the beginning again, organizing it better, but, of course, you remember me as a lazy student, and I have to admit that this is my fifteenth attempt to write you, believe it or not. I knew that if I began this letter for the sixteenth time, I would write it in exactly the same way—with no order and totally confused, but I am sure you will understand anyway. So, as I told you, I am no longer even a priest. Now I am a botanist, I study flowers. The last letter I sent to you at the old address in Rijnsburg was written on the day I discovered a new flower previously unknown in botany. You were—or rather, that letter was—the first to know about my discovery, though I do not approve of the use of the word *discovery* in botany when we find a flower previously unknown to us, since flowers have known about themselves since the moment they were created; we only find them. I often remember that winter morning when you told me something about Descartes, I do not remember what exactly. Ah, I would like to tear this letter apart right this minute and start it once again, because I do not want it to say that I no longer remembered exactly what you told me, but believe me, it is not because I did not want to remember it—I wanted so much to remember everything you told me—but it was simply extremely difficult for me to understand all those things. Ah, yes, here is what I wanted to write you about. While you spoke to me then, I told you to step back, since I had a feeling that under the snow where you stood there was a flower, and it was indeed so. I think it was then that I came to love plants so much. If it were not for that event with you, I might have been a philosopher or a priest until the end of my days. I would have been a bad philosopher or a bad priest, and now I am perhaps a good botanist. Dear Mr. Spinoza, forgive me if this letter is too tedious or commonplace or ordinary, but I know that you will understand me; as you can see, this time I am not referring to Descartes' philosophy or preaching about the deeds of Jesus; it would be unforgivable for a person like me to write such a letter. I have, for a long time, been just a man who observes the life of plants and who sometimes, in his sleep, dreams that he has a root or a flower instead of a head. Such dreams make me happy. I know, you are laughing while you read this, and I would really like to make you laugh at this very moment if with nothing else but the simplicity of my existence, which to any citizen of the Dutch Kingdom might seem vain and meaningless. This kind of life, however, brings me a quiet joy that is as warm as the wind that blows from the ocean. This is all I wanted to write to you about, dear Mr. Spinoza. And yet, I also wanted to write you about something else. In fact, from the very beginning of this letter I wanted to write you about this thing. Maybe you still remember the night before the morning you sent me away. It is strange, but after that night (you have probably forgotten that that night you spoke to me about infinity), yes, after that night, I became obsessed with infinity. I cannot find the words to describe the feeling. I was simply looking at my hand and wondered why it did not extend to infinity. When I went to bed, I looked at my toes and imagined them extending farther and farther, piercing the wall and leaving the town. I imagined my toes leaving the Netherlands and continuing where the globe becomes rounded to form a circular line. My toes extended as far as the sky, traveled there, beside the stars, and then penetrated the sky itself, going beyond it, entering infinity. . . . I wanted to arrive at the ultimate point of finiteness, to the utmost limits, I wanted to see where infinity began, and all of this was because of your words, Mr. Spinoza, because of your conviction that anything that has borders is not worthy of devoting our lives to. Hence I decided to travel to India. I thought, Ah, yes, it must be the ultimate point on earth; the earth could not extend farther than India. How stupid I was, I am probably just as stupid now, but now I have one more significant piece of knowledge. It is here that I have discovered where finiteness begins. I realized that finiteness is infinite. Believe me, when I lie on the ground in the evening, watching the sky—and the sky looks so low here—it seems to me that a star might drop onto my face. It is this closeness that tells me that everything is distant and infinite, Mr. Spinoza. Yes, this is what I wanted to write to you about, and this is all I had to tell you. So, in case you have not forgotten me, and if you find time, and, of course, if it is not too mortifying for you to reply to this letter, please write me how you are, what you are thinking, and whether perhaps you would like to see the Indian Ocean.

Your humble servant,
Johannes Casearius

There were three pressed flowers between the four paper sheets. The letter arrived a little late at your address—a few days after you were buried. Johannes Casearius waited for your reply until one Thursday, later in the summer of that year, someone sent him a letter informing him of your death. After that, Johannes's enormously long body from his dreams that extended far beyond the sky, to infinity, began diminishing: initially to the limits of the sky, then to the nearest star, and then continued to diminish even more. After a while, the ends of his toes reached only to the middle of the Indian Ocean, then to the coastline, and finally merely to the pollen grain of a flower near his home. And it was not ordained that his body diminished only in his dreams but also in reality. That same year he fell ill with dysentery, and he died one warm autumn night, gazing into the low skies over Malabar. He is remembered in botany for the plant *Casearia* Jacq. from the Flacourtiaceae family, which he discovered and which was named after him.

What happened then, Spinoza? Did your struggle against affections continue even after Johannes had left? Did affections continue to pursue you while you strived to come closer to the third type of knowledge?

An Explanation of the Sharpness of the Blade

No, after that everything changed. My daily life consisted of waking up at dawn, reading René Descartes and Giordano Bruno, grinding lenses, writing, and going to bed two hours before midnight. I did not suffer from insomnia anymore, though I continued to forget my dreams shortly before I woke up. My existence turned into drawing the most accurate geometric forms in which, owing to the perfection of the lines, you could no longer discern the hand of the draftsman. I lived life less and less, and I wrote more and more philosophy. My hope was no longer to live with Clara Maria one day. Hope was now just a definition, a fickle joy, the consequence of an image of a past or future action whose outcome we doubt. Fear for me was no longer a fear of the question *What then?* but fickle sorrow, the consequence of a past or future action whose outcome we doubt.

I am telling you, _____, that it was no longer life, it was just the habitual writing of philosophy. It was as if you were attempting to explain the sharpness of the blade instead of experiencing that sharpness on your own veins.

■ □ ■ □ ■

So nothing would disturb your geometric precision, nothing would draw the blade closer to your flesh—so that you might truly experience hope once again, and not only as a definition, so that your fear would not be just a fickle sorrow, the consequence of a past or future action whose outcome we doubt? So even if you had met Clara Maria, it would have had no effect on your habitual existence, on your philosophical contemplation of life?

■ □ ■ □ ■

No, it would have had no effect, none at all. I met Clara Maria in 1663, when her father wrote some pamphlets against the state. They knew I could no longer visit their home since it would have been an additional burden for me: I had already been proclaimed a man who spoke on behalf of the devil.

It might have been the last time we saw each other. She stood there leaning on the balcony balustrade, looking into the distance, toward the horizon. I tried to remember her, to remember how she looked on that occasion, but even then, let alone later, when I attempted to remember those moments, I repeat, even then, _____, I could not visualize her outward appearance. Her voice and the smell of her breath had escaped me like water flowing through my fingers (I could not recall if she smelled of the freshest milk). I was not even sure whether her eyes looked like they did before: questioning amazement in one of them and omniscience in the other. I was totally immersed in my own bewilderment. I knew that this might be the last time we saw each other, and she was also aware of that.

"Is this the last time we will see each other?" she asked.

"Maybe," I said.

"Are you sad?" she asked.

"Sadness is only an affection. And there is no affection from which we cannot create an adequate idea—when a certain body does not agree with ours and affects us with sadness, we can create an idea about what that body and our body have in common."

"What then?"

"In this way we can understand why these bodies do not agree with each other—any human can understand why his own body and the external body cannot combine their relationships in a permanent way."

"What then?"

"This knowledge brings joy. Once we understand the causes of our sadness, sadness ceases to be suffering."

"What then?"

"The positive joy that stems from the creation of an adequate idea of sadness leads us to the creation of more and more adequate ideas about everything that surrounds us. In this way we can acquire adequate ideas about divine attributes."

"What then?"

"Then our knowledge goes from the adequate idea about some divine attributes to learning about the essence of things. It is in this way that we inform our knowledge about the eternal essences—our knowledge about the divine essence, about individual essences such as they are in God and such as they are understood in God."

"What then?"

"Then there's nothing more. This is the final achievement."

"You don't understand me at all. You always answer my questions as if I were asking you, *What about reason then?* But I'm, in fact, asking you, *What about life then?*"

Now I believe that not only did I not understand her then but that I have never understood her. That misunderstanding, however, did not come from a lack of a desire on my part to understand her, but from my fear that I might understand her. I asked myself, "What about philosophy?" while she asked herself, "What about life?" Life had a frightening significance for me; philosophy without life was meaningless to her.

"What about life?" The words of her question echoed in my mind. I could feel the words hurting me in the chest.

"Yes," she said. She noticed how I felt. Although her desire was to see everything that I said come to dust, she did not want me to feel like a loser. She did not want me to look like a loser, although deep inside she knew that I had lost the most important battle. She knew that I had transformed my life into a battle to reach the eternal and the infinite. She turned to the sunlight that blinded her eyes, lest she see the changes on my face.

"Life goes along the path it is guided to by reason," I said, knowing that she noticed the change in my voice—the sound of self-confidence with which I tried to disguise my sadness, which was anyway betrayed by the gaps between my sentences. Once I felt that my breathing had become completely calm again, I added: "As far as my life is concerned, I know exactly what I am to do in the future: I will continue to aspire toward and gain knowledge of what is eternal."

"So you'll try to forget this meeting of ours as soon as possible, as it is condemned to be transient. It took place"—and she looked at the clock tower—"between eleven and eleven-thirty-five one normal morning, as impermanent as any other. You'll try to forget this conversation, a little unusual indeed, as it referred to eternity, but nonetheless was transient. You'll try to forget me, who may carry on for a few decades to come, but compared to eternity, it is as brief as the life of the mayfly, which is born in the morning, sees the first purple colors of dawn, and then dies with the disappearance of the last blue shades of the dusk. But isn't this the greatest defiance you could possibly demonstrate vis-à-vis eternity—to squeeze your own existence into a day? And, of course, together with this morning, this conversation, and me, you'll also try to forget yourself. At least that part of you that is transient," she said. Then she turned, pushed the curtain aside, and went into the house.

In the past, when she left me, the smell of her body, the smell of the freshest milk remained there, elements of the sounds that filled her words remained in the room, her movements remained in the air. I could see her, in the empty space, turning toward the window or arranging her hair. Her look remained there, harnessing my pupils to her absentminded but sparkling eyes. Now only her bitterness remained behind, pushing me toward the balcony balustrade, while I struggled in vain to remember her outward appearance.

■ □ ■ □ ■

The clock tower strikes twelve, and you are still standing on the balcony. Franciscus van den Enden approaches and you say to him:
"I have to go."
"Will you come again?" he asks you.
You shrug your shoulders. While Franciscus talks to you, you do not listen to his words; you are thinking that as soon as you get to Rijnsburg, you will have to pack your things and move to Voorburg.

■ □ ■ □ ■

That first night in Voorburg I could not sleep at all. I left the candle lit and stared for a long time at the crack in the wall. When the candle went out, I did not get up to light a new one. Lying in bed, I just stretched out my hand, opened the wooden window shutter, and watched the shadows on the wall created by the clouds passing in the sky and covering the full moon. With the approach of the morning, when my eyes had finally begun to close, I heard someone walking slowly by outside. Hearing the steps, I knew that one of the legs of this person was shorter than the other. Half asleep, I suddenly thought that it was Clara Maria coming to visit me. I jumped out of bed and looked through the window—an old woman was walking slowly past, limping.

Then I moved to The Hague. The unbearable lightness of my meticulous being continued unabated, especially after some of my friends had died.

The streets are empty, only my steps are destroying the feeling that time has stood still. Had I not been moving, had I stood on the same spot, it would have seemed that I was looking at a painter's canvas depicting a dead city. A dog's barking can be heard in one of the neighboring streets, and then, all of a sudden, the barking is lost to human voices, and then the human voices become mixed with the dog's yelping. I look at the windows of the houses: you can see several people in at least one window of each house. In the beginning, it gives you a feeling that the city is unusually alive, but as I move on, the more people I see behind the closed windows, the stronger my impression that they are somehow frozen. The people are not looking at each other, they are not talking to each other, only the blinking of their eyes indicates that they are alive. They are standing there motionless and mute inside the window frames as if in some kind of a group portrait painted by an incompetent painter who has portrayed their faces too pale and rigid.

A dog is heard from somewhere. The doors of the houses begin to open, people are running out of their homes, making an unbearable noise. An old woman with a wild look and a twisted mouth runs close to me and hits me with the broomstick she is holding in her hands.

"Catch the villain!" she shouts and runs alongside a group of people who are chasing after a dog that tries to escape but finds himself surrounded.

"Kill the beast!" echoes through the winter air. The phrase is being repeated like a refrain, while the circle around the frightened dog is becoming smaller. The people hold brooms, clubs, or oars in their hands, and everyone tries to hit the dog with whatever they have. The dog gathers courage and runs into the circle surrounding him. A few women scream and the circle is broken. The dog begins to run away down the street.

"Kill the beast!" the refrain is shouted and is repeated by the chorus. Other people come running out of their houses where the dog is passing, holding spades, clubs, and oars. The old woman with the wild look and twisted mouth, who hit me a little earlier with her broomstick, slides on the ice and falls. Her broom hovers in the air for just a moment and then it falls too, hitting the old woman's bottom.

"Kill the beast!" she cries, although the crowd is now far away from her and too noisy to hear anything.

I can see a crowd near the end of the street hitting the dog. A boy, who has virtually no forehead, with his hairline beginning just above his eyebrows, hits the dog's tail with the end of his oar. The dog squeals and, not knowing where to go, runs directly into the man who holds a spade in his hand and who strikes the animal ferociously on his head. The furious crowd attacks the dog and hits him until the last squeal is heard, a protracted sound full of pain. A hunchbacked old man, who, from what I remember, used to beg close to the churches and synagogues when I was a child, grabs the dead dog and puts him into a bag. Then he snatches the ropes at the end of the bag and begins to pull the bag over the snow. While he passes by the old woman who is still struggling to get up, she clutches her broomstick and hits the bag fiercely.

"This is from me, you beast!"

The dog everyone believed to be dead squeals once again, for the last time.

"He's a real beast, still alive!" growls the old woman, whom a few people are helping to get up.

I follow the old man who pulls the bag behind him. People are still standing in the windows of the houses we pass by. They are still quite stiff at first, but seeing what the old man is pulling in his bag, strange smiles appear on their faces. We get to the square. There is a heap of bags. A man talks to the old man, hands him some money, and the old man throws the bag on the heap. Then the old man and a dozen other beggars climb up the heap and pour tar on it. One of them lights a bag and the fire quickly spreads to all of them. Some of the dogs that are not yet dead begin to squeal, and I close my ears. Had it been possible not to breathe, I would have closed my nose too. I can already smell the awful stench in the air. I take my fingers from my ears and begin to walk away from the square. The dogs' squeals are now weaker than the sound of the clock tower. It strikes twelve.

I go back to the home of Simon de Vries and ask him about what I have seen.

"Every day at twelve they burn dogs in the square, and then the whole city stinks of tar and burned meat until midnight. Someone has told the people that dogs transmit the plague," he said, giving a pat to his own dog.

"That's why I'm not letting him out this winter."

These were the years when the plague returned to Amsterdam. Ten thousand people died in 1663, and twenty-five thousand the following year—every seventh inhabitant of the city perished from the pestilence.

The next day I went back to The Hague, and a month later I learned that Simon had died. After his death I had a burning desire to go to the cemetery where my parents were buried.

As I was walking between the graves, I felt my steps becoming slower and my legs heavier. I looked for the places where Mother, Father, and Isaac were buried. I remembered that there was a tall tree near the grave of Father, while the graves of Mother and Isaac were just a little below, toward the river. I expected their graves to be among those overgrown by weed. I moved the weed away from the grave slabs near the trees, hoping to read the name MICHAEL SPINOZA on one of them. I found my father's name on a grave under a tall tree. I started to weed the plants, to clean the grave, and then went on a few steps toward the river: there were two graves lying side by side. When I pulled out the weeds covering the slabs, I was able to read HANNA DEBORAH SPINOZA on one of them and ISAAC SPINOZA on the other. I felt that my body was moving faster than ever while I quickly pulled the weeds out. Their stems cut my palms and fingers, making them bleed. Then I went to the riverbank. I took one of the buckets people used to wash the graves of their kin, filled it with water, and returned to where Hanna, Isaac, and Michael were buried. I lifted the bucket to wash one of the graves, but my hands shook. The bucket fell from my hands, and the water splashed everywhere, including over my feet. I was exhausted; I sat on Mother's grave, and I had an odd feeling, as if something distant and forgotten was beginning to come back to me. It was not a specific event, it was just a feeling, obviously an affection that I had not defined in my *Ethics* and whose name I did not know. I felt a need to clench my hands into fists, put them on my chest, and then bend my body, relax my neck, and let my head fall forward. Then I simply let my head rest on my hands. I wondered what kind of feeling it was. I could not come up with an answer. It was not sorrow, or despair, or anger. It was a combined feeling, a combined affection—it was some kind of transition. It seemed to me that I even experienced the taste of irreversible transience, a taste I had for the first time in many, many years. At the same time, it seemed to me that that transience took the form of everything around me and that it was only I who did not belong there and that it was precisely at that moment that that form both covered me and penetrated into me, swallowing my body and my existence, making me cry after so many years, for the first time after Mother died.

After a while I took a boat to Amsterdam, where I wanted to see the house where I was born.

The house was not the same anymore. No orange paint was peeling off; it was painted red instead. I might never have recognized it if not for the carob trees that had been cut down only in front of our house. The door was different as well. I knocked, and an old blind man appeared from behind it.

"Is this the home of Gabriel Spinoza, sir?"

"I'm very sorry, sir," he said. "I came here a year ago with the family of my son, and I don't speak Dutch or any other language except Spanish. And Hebrew, of course."

"Is this the home of Gabriel Spinoza?" I asked him in Spanish.

"It may have been, but it certainly isn't any longer," replied the old man. "A man used to live here who ran a shop selling spices, dried fruit, and wine. I heard his voice before he left. It was a slow voice, but at the same time, the words he uttered seemed to glide around so effortlessly."

"Do you have any idea where he is now?"

"I believe he said he was setting off to some distant island. I think the name was Barbados or Brabados. That's what he said. Please, do come in, sir," he said. "You can look around the house, if you want to," and he beckoned me in with his hand, inviting me to come in, while his blind pupils stared somewhere over my head.

I stepped into the house. The smell of our home was gone.

"They've told me this was," he said, showing me the mirror, "the only thing left from the family who lived here before; the rest was sold. Yes, it is here, I can feel its smooth surface."

I looked at myself in the mirror: my face was smeared with soil. I turned away from the mirror, I could not bear to look at myself, and I took a couple of steps back.

"You, sir, you obviously come from Spain too. Your Spanish is excellent."

"No," I said, "I was born right here," and it occurred to me that I stood exactly on the spot where the large red-canopied bed once stood, the bed in which I was born.

"So you were born in Amsterdam, but your parents must have come from Spain then, that's what I meant," said the old man, smiling and running his hand across his head. "I rarely meet people who speak Spanish here. As a matter of fact, I rarely meet any people at all. My son is a merchant, and his wife and children died from the plague, you know. My son leaves early in the morning to go to work and comes back late in the evening," he said and, groping, found a chair to sit on. "You know, if you want to, you can buy the mirror. . . . No, I'll give it to you for free. I don't need it anymore, and neither does my son."

My eyes began turning toward the mirror, but swiftly moved back and looked into the old man's flickering pupils.

"No, thank you," I said. "I already have a mirror."

"But this one is indeed beautiful," said the old man. "I sometimes touch it. When I'm sad, when I'm alone, when I remember how far I am from Spain and from everything that used to be my life, knowing that I've lost my sight forever—and even if I hadn't, I know I could no longer see what I want to see—it is then that I come to this mirror," he said, getting up from his chair and approaching the mirror. "It is then that I touch it," he added, putting his fingers on the smooth surface. "Just feel this, sir, how smooth it is. Please, touch it." He was seeking my hand with his free hand, and I offered it to him. He took my fingers and put them on the mirror. I looked at them. "Just think, sir, how many faces have appeared in this mirror. They are no longer on its surface or inside it, but they have nonetheless left some traces. I can feel this, I can feel them at the ends of my fingers. Can you feel the remnants of these reflections with your fingers?" He sighed. "I miss my sight, sir. But I'm still grateful to God that I can still touch, smell, hear, and taste. Imagine what a painful world it would be if there existed only ideas. Imagine a world without sight, hearing, touch, taste, or smell. A world with only ideas passing each other. And mind you, they just pass each other, they do not touch each other, they know nothing about each other. Ideas that can neither see each other nor hear or utter the words of other ideas; they cannot touch each other, smell each other, or taste each other. It would be a very . . . a very . . . " The old man strove to find the appropriate words. "It would be a world, sir, it would be a world for which I cannot find a name. For I am blind, and those ideas are also blind to each other. I would rather call that world a sad world, but that world cannot be sad, since sadness comes only after we've known something different, something that is part of the non-*I*. My sadness comes from the fact that through touch, taste, hearing, and smell I know that there is something that is part of the non-*I*, and in specific situations this awareness about the non-*I* makes me sad. That world couldn't be sad, sir, because those ideas would know nothing about each other. But could they know anything about themselves if they know nothing about other ideas?" The old man stopped, taking his fingers off the mirror. "I'm very sorry, sir. I'm talking too much, perhaps. You know, I used to teach philosophy and mysticism to young Jews in Spain, but that was a long time ago. . . ." He blushed like a child. "But please, take this mirror. I really think you should take it, sir. I felt something very unusual passing through your hand when I put your fingers on its surface. . . ."

I noticed that my fingers were still on the mirror.

"I really have to go, sir," I said and I brought my hand close to my body.

"Please, stay a little more. I know I can be tiresome, at least that's what my son tells me when someone comes into the house and I start talking. I'm always saying the same things, and you've told me nothing about yourself, you haven't even told me how you managed to learn Spanish so well, being born here."

"My father and mother came from Portugal," I said, "and I studied in Spanish here."

"Why don't you sit down, sir, just for a minute or two?" said the old man, indicating the direction in which he supposed there was a chair. "I have to go," I said. "I no longer live here." I looked at the stairs leading to the attic rooms. "I no longer live in Amsterdam."

"Where do you live now, sir? But please, do sit down. . . ."

"I live in The Hague," I replied, and then I looked over my shoulder into the mirror. It appeared to me that I saw my face from the past, as if I were looking at myself in the mirror for the first time. I saw the same flabbergasted face from when I was five. "But why don't you live in Amsterdam anymore?" asked the old man. "I don't know," I answered. Suddenly the confused face of my childhood was lost, and behind it appeared my face as I looked into the mirror for the last time, that night when, immediately after my excommunication, I left home. I was looking at my curved eyebrows, the sharpness of my eyes, the reserved smile. "Now that I'm blind, it's all the same to me where I live," said the old man. The deathbed of my mother seemed to appear in the mirror with myself close to her. I saw myself looking at her dead eyes in the mirror, I felt as if I was losing something at that very moment, or becoming aware of something that had been lost to me many years before; it was like the rediscovery of a feeling that had been lost long ago. "I'm sorry, sir, I talk too much, and you have nothing to say to me, this is probably not very interesting for you. . . ."

"No, that's not true," I said with a changed voice. A strange and heavy heat seemed to have descended down my throat and melted all the words I wanted to say. "But I really have to go," I said as I turned to leave.

■ □ ■ □ ■

The old man follows you. He thinks he was boring you, that he went too far with his explanations and questions. He knows nothing, but his assumptions may have been right. You leave the house, and he comes to the door. "Take this mirror, sir," he says, but you cannot hear him; you are walking on with haste down the street. He makes another two or three steps after you, and then stops. He walks back into his home, sidling along the walls, mumbling something about the mirror. You leave for The Hague that evening, never again to return to Amsterdam.

THREAD FIVE

■ □ ■ □ ■

THREAD SIX

Watching

As soon as I got back to my room in The Hague, I looked at myself in the mirror. For the first time after so many years I was looking at myself in the mirror. Until then, I only looked in the mirror to see if my hair was tidy, or if I had sleep in my eyes, or if I had a white moustache on my lips after drinking my morning milk. Now I was again looking at myself, and it was as though I were seeing my face for the first time. I resembled someone standing on the edge of something: it was neither a safe expanse, nor was I falling into an abyss—I was only standing at the edge. That is how I appeared in the mirror. I began touching my face, then I smelled my palms and bit strands of my hair, then I said E and listened to my voice, then I said M and listened to my voice, then I said P and listened to my voice, then I said T and listened to my voice, then I said Y and listened to my voice, and then I involuntarily let out a long drawn-out scream, something that was hard for me to hear, and I saw myself falling, touching the floor, and then breathing in dust.

I was overwhelmed by a profound fear of things past. I wanted to remember everything that had happened in the past, to seal it in somehow, to preserve it. I remembered things that used to be and that were no more. I tried to touch, see, smell, taste, and hear once again in my memory everything that had existed at one time.

I came to look for comfort in the remnants of the past.

As long as my memory is preserved, Clara Maria will be brushing away the strands of her hair that fell across her face, and Johannes will be laughing on the little chair close to my bed. I sometimes cannot remember whether the air around their bodies was moving or standing still. I cannot remember in what way the air around them was moving, in what way it was standing still. There are moments when I cannot see Johannes's eyes inside my closed eyes. I see him as if he were on a painter's canvas—he is moving, but someone has cut his eyes out. I sometimes cannot hear the voice of Clara Maria in my memory. I repeat her words to myself, but her voice eludes all my attempts to capture it. Forgotten things hurt me, oblivion hurts me. I, who used to believe that remembrance is just an unnecessary preservation of sensory imprints from the past, am now sitting in a corner of my room trying to remember the color of Clara Maria's voice when she asked me, "What then?" I am no longer straining to hear that voice again through my ears, but inside my ears, in my memory, so I shut my ears with my index fingers. I try to see Johannes again, walking toward me, to see his smile, the hand he put on my shoulder. I try to see all that again through closed eyes, to feel his touch. Forgotten things hurt me, those traces of outward appearance erased from my memory. Yet some things are still there, and they fill my day between waking up and going to sleep. An event suddenly emerges from my memory while I am having breakfast with the Spyck family; a pair of gentle eyes is looking at me while the shopgirl is handing me a loaf of bread; I later realize that my journey into remembrance has transferred Clara Maria's gentle eyes onto the eyes of the baker woman. In the Broken Horn tavern, I stare at the table absentmindedly and then see Johannes's strong arm serving me a glass of wine; I lift my head and I notice the stooping old man who has always served there; I again gaze into his hand; it is no longer Johannes's hand, but a dry old man's hand. I go back home, I look at the white wall, and I can see the past there too. Yes, this is what fills my day. I can sometimes even see Clara Maria's eyelashes, I can see them in my memory much closer than I saw them in reality, I can see them from a very small distance, less than the cross section of a hair away from my eyes. I can see Johannes's hairline; then I try to remember at least some of the movements of Johannes's body, like the running of his fingers through his hair, or walking to the door, and I repeat those movements in my memory again and again: he runs his fingers through his hair thousands of times or walks to the door thousands of times. I pull all the events back to my memory, then I try to get closer to all the smells, all the touches and movements that I missed, without even realizing that they were there, without experiencing them then and there.

I sometimes wish to know how something that had not even begun would have turned out. While I am passing by other people's homes in the evening, I look inside their windows and think: what if it were possible to see through this window all the things that might have happened but have never happened, what if it were possible to see through this window the continuance of all the events that ended even before they had begun? I stop in front of those windows, having learned how to efface the human figures on the other side of the glass: a husband, a wife, and three children are having dinner; one of the children refuses to eat the soup, the father slaps him on the face, but I am telling you, _____, I do not see all that; only the window, the frame, remains, and inside there is a canvas with unexplored possibilities. Clara Maria appears in the frame, I am there too, we are having dinner, she and I; children appear from time to time and come close to us; then they disappear, and then reappear, and disappear again; they do not enter into or go out of the window frame, but seem to be created from the air and disappear back into it. Clara Maria asks me if it is indeed impossible to learn anything through the senses. "Everything," I answer, "everything can be learned through the senses." She lifts her dress a little, she spreads her legs, and I can see the pinkness of her crotch. I am bending my head down, I am caressing her with my tongue; it is infinitely warm there, yes, it is infinitely warm; it is only now that I can experience the essence of the word *infinite* (although I have known its meaning for a long time now with the help of reason). Now, while I am shivering in the cold on this side of the window and imagining how there, on the other side, my tongue is going over the infinite warm areas of her crotch, and everything that comes to pass afterward—the touches, the movements, the sounds produced by our throats, the merging of our bodies—it is like going back home, like coming back to the perfect home you left even before you were born. At a certain moment the expression on Clara Maria's face changes, she is putting her finger on my lips, she is turning toward the window and tells me, "Our children are watching us." I am turning too, I am looking through the window, and there, on the other side, I can see myself standing and shivering in the cold. And again, I become that person who, in the cold of the night, looks through someone else's window, and in that window there is no Clara Maria, there is no me, there is not even the family that dined together—the candles have been put out. I am suddenly roused from my reverie, thinking that a passerby who will see me peeping into someone else's window may appear in the street, and I continue my walk, stepping into the darkness. Sometimes I go back home immediately, but sometimes, when my legs do not hurt too much, I continue walking for a long time.

I come back to the house of the Spyck family. None of the windows are lit; everyone is asleep. I go into the house, come to the door of my room, but I do not enter it. I kneel and look through the keyhole: I can see Johannes inside, but he looks unusually big to me, and yet about the same size as he was. I am also there. "What shall we do with our limitations?" he asks me. "You are infinite," I tell him. I am touching that infinity between his legs in a way I have never touched the infinity of substance, and then that infinity is entering into me. At the moment when it seems to me that I am entirely overwhelmed by such infinity, only the keyhole remains before my eye: I can no longer see myself and Johannes inside—only my empty bed.

I am shaken by the change of view. I stand up and go into my room. I go to bed.

I sometimes love to watch Clara Maria dreaming. I do not want to see her everyday reality, I do not want to see her waking up in the morning, I do not want to see her looking at Theodor to find out if he is awake or still asleep, I do not want to know if she wishes to be away from him or to be with him all the time, I do not want to know if the smell of his body is repulsive to her or whether, while he is away, she keeps some of his clothes close to herself, bringing them close to her nostrils from time to time, I do not want to see how she walks barefoot around the room, I do not want to see her washing herself, sitting in front of the mirror, looking directly into her pupils—not wishing to see the expression on her face, I do not want to see the expression on her face, I do not want to judge by this expression whether she is sad or happy while she looks into her pupils because there is something inside them that is beyond any sadness or happiness, and is sadder and happier than both, I do not want to see her running the comb through her long hair illuminated by the sun's rays, I do not want to see her gazing into the clouds reflected in the mirror, I do not want to see her having breakfast with Theodor, I do not want to hear what they are talking about, nor do I want to know if they are talking at all, I do not want to see her rolling up her sleeves to wash the dishes after he leaves the house, I do not want to see her then going up to the attic rooms, standing in front of the window and gazing long into the distance, somewhere across the street, over the houses, across the city, and even beyond, beyond the horizon, I do not want to see her leaving the window open, coming toward the bed, putting her elbows on her lap and putting her head in her hands, her hair falling down below her knees, the curtains fluttering in the wind, the sheets floating up, and yet everything being so dead in that room, just like in mine, I do not want to know why she sits motionless like that for hours, I do not want to know if it is painful for her not to have any children, thinking that she will never have them, or if it is the purposelessness of existence that is painful to her, I do not want to know if she feels the pain of all the sentences she has read in books, I do not want to know if she feels the burning of all the thoughts that cannot come out of her, having no one to share them with, like swallowed needles pricking the stomach; then she hears someone knocking at the door, she knows it is the milkwoman, she wipes her eyes, runs down the stairs, takes off the latch, opens the door, and takes two bottles of milk. I do not want to see her going back to the music room with a sigh, reaching for an instrument—it is only a half-movement, just an attempt—and then, suddenly, pulling her hand back close to her body. I do not want to know if the echoes of the compositions she has played in the past resound in her ears at those moments. Then she leaves the room and goes to the market. I am sure she always buys sweet things, dried figs and raisins, honey and strawberry preserves, but I do not want to know all this, I do not want to know how she walks through the out-of-the-way streets and then continues on to the outskirts of the city, asking herself until she is completely exhausted who she is, replying that she is Clara Maria, gathering leaves and putting them in her pockets in autumn, gathering small flowers in springtime. She then returns home, and before going in, she remembers that somewhere on the outskirts of the city she has forgotten the dried figs, honey, and strawberry preserves. I do not want to see how she crosses the threshold, while Theodor sees her from the other end of the room and says to her, "Your nose is red," and she says to herself, "And my fingers frozen." Yet she does not put her fingers on his cheeks, she goes to the bookshelves, touches book after book and remembers our game, but I do not want to know if, going through the books, she still recites a sentence from each of them, I do not want to see the smile on her face while she plays this game, nor do I want to see how sadness overwhelms her face as soon as she becomes aware of her smile, remembering what has aroused it in the first place, taking a book, *The Anatomy of Melancholy*—the book opens by itself on the page where it has often been opened and read—and then reading: "*I live a living death, my flesh is wounded, bleeding, cadaverized, my rhythm slowed down or interrupted, time has been erased or blotted, absorbed into sorrow.*" I do not want to know what she loves and what she hates, nor do I want to know what her hopes are or what her fears are, I do not want to know if she feels a desire in the evening to touch Theodor's body, or if she hates sleeping beside him, I do not want to see if she puts her legs around his body with pleasure, or if she does it with trepidation and disgust, or if there is distance between their bodies, as there is between their souls. I do not want to know if she remembers me at those moments, whether she remembers that night in my room, on the canopied bed, when she asked me if anything could be learned by touch, smell, taste, hearing, and sight, I do not want to know if she remembers the smell of my semen the night when she smelled Theodor's semen for the first time, and if she thought that I had been lying to her that night when we were together, or more importantly, lying to myself, when I desired Clara Maria's transience. I do not want to see her struggling with her insomnia, I do not want to see her trying to get some sleep. I want to watch her sleeping. And I am looking at her sleeping, her head eagerly awaiting the approaching dream, and I am imagining her dream. I want her dreams to be filled with a lot of blue, I want her dreams to smell of the freshest milk. I do not know why, but what really matters to me in her dreams are colors and smells. What happens in them is totally irrelevant to me; it does not matter if, while I am imagining Clara Maria's dreams, I see her holding ashes in her left hand and squeezing the head of a fish with her right hand, opening its mouth and pouring ashes into it, after which

I see her swallowing the fish and plunging into the sky, nor do I pay any attention to the large rope whose ends she ties around the necks of two identical bodies, identical to my body, and then she takes her own body off and begins to walk the rope without a body, from one of my heads to the other, and vice versa. The only thing that really matters to me in these dreams is that they begin in the color blue, continue in red, and end with the smell of the freshest milk. So every morning when I wake up, when I try to recall what I have dreamed during the brief hours I had some sleep, when I become aware that I can remember nothing, I begin to think of her, I see her turning her face toward the wall and beginning to dream in blue.

I also want to know where Johannes is and what he is doing. Is he still looking for flowers under the snow, and is he still riding limited, finite things? I want to know what his first thought after waking up is: is there a man or a woman close to him when he wakes up? I want to know if he has a son and if he explains to him the meaning of the word *fly,* if he still remembers the dead bird he saw on the road that noon when he left. I want to know if he teaches his son to ride and whether, having concluded that all his efforts have been in vain, he now thinks: "He'll be like Professor Benedictus Spinoza. Anyone will be able to tell by his walk that he's not a rider." I want to see him, after every sunset, gazing into the dusk and asking himself: "Does infinity really exist?"

I am thinking of how forcefully I have driven everybody away from me for the sake of this *I*—myself.

What *I,* which *I*? *I* where from and *I* where to? Why *I*? But, above all, what *I*? This *I* who rubs his sweaty hands in his pockets on this winter morning? This *I* who walks along the road leading out of The Hague going to the plains, where the blueness of dawn tumbles across the snowy fields? What *I,* that *I* of Spinoza who gazes into the patterns made by the flocks of birds in the gray sky? What *I,* that of myself who walks behind the trails of a horse-driven vehicle in the snow and watches the hoofprints of the two horses that have driven it, and then stares at the steam coming out of his own nostrils while breathing out? Where can you find that *I,* while I am remembering the morning when my mother explained to me the meanings of *inhale* and *exhale,* and I am wondering: was that *I* really this *I*? I take some snow and make a snowball. The cold of the snow reminds me of the coldness of Clara Maria's fingers, which she once put on my cheeks, saying: "Feel how cold they are." Was that *I* really this *I* who tried to warm up Clara Maria's frozen fingers with my breath? I throw the snowball as far as I can, and I continue along the road—the wind blows in my face and makes me close my eyes, just as I closed them one cool summer night wondering what to do next, after my excommunication, while I was walking in the streets of Amsterdam, just as I closed them one morning when I told Johannes that he had to leave and go back to Leiden, just as I closed them cleaning Father's grave.

Which *I* should you choose among all those *I*'s split in time and scattered throughout space? Or perhaps you should turn your face away from all that splitting and scattering, and start the other way round, look for one integrated *I* that perhaps exists vis-à-vis all those separate *I*'s, not somewhere on the opposite side of the wind, but where there are no opposite sides and no wind, where neither time nor space exist.

Or, this *I* is, after all, within all those *I*'s, within all those past *I*'s; this *I* is in the child who listens to the meanings of *inhale* and *exhale* explained by his mother for the first time; this *I* is also in his mother's words, this *I* is also in the inhaling and the exhaling. This *I* is in my cheeks and also in Clara Maria's fingers on these cheeks, and also in her words, "Feel how cold they are." This *I* is in the man who had to leave his home and then walked through the streets of Amsterdam, this *I* is in the man who forced Johannes to leave, and also in the man who cleaned the graves overgrown with weeds.

But how to arrive at that moment when all those *I*'s will be united, how can you attain that moment of union? I know, although this moment seems impossible to reach, I know that it is then that I will achieve what I have always wanted to achieve, it is then that I will touch a part of eternity and infinity; perhaps since experiencing all things past and irreversible, I will be more aware than ever of the vexing pain of transience and finiteness.

Along the road I come upon a duck that has fallen into the snow and frozen to death. I turn back—the misty winter sun slowly rises above the rooftops in The Hague. I am on my way back to the city.

And then there were mornings of a different kind: there were days when despair was the only thing I could feel. I could sense those days coming; like animals foretelling an accident, I had a presentiment of them coming nearer and nearer. I would then buy a bottle of milk, a few loaves of bread, and tobacco and lock myself up in my room. The Spycks knew about this habit of mine and did not disturb me. I would remain there alone for several days, being perhaps closer to myself and closer to others than at any other time. On such days I did not even try to run away from my memories, exchange them for adequate ideas, or think about God and develop an intellectual love for him. At such times I thought of the finger of a young girl running her finger over my back like a falling leaf, of that night with Clara Maria when I was only a step away from becoming something different from what I was during the solitary hours of self-torture. I remembered the smell of her body. I remembered Johannes's voice, the strange tones that filled my penis with blood, the form of his body. On days like these, and even more so, on nights like these, since despair did not let me sleep, I sat in one of the corners of the room, changing corners every three hours, so that I sat twice in each corner during one day and one night. On such days and nights, it was only the corners that seemed to at least offer me some kind of protection, the only space where I could sit with no fear of disappearing altogether. On those days and nights, I was frightened to think about going out and walking in the street, or even leaving the room. I was afraid that I might fall into a space where there was no existence, where everything moved toward its end, and, what was most frightening of all, where no infinite substance existed. On such days and nights, I left the corners of the room only occasionally, only to go to the middle of the room and have a sip of milk, a bite of bread, or a pinch of chewing tobacco. I sometimes went to my table for grinding lenses, but I did not go there to work, I just wanted to touch the glass dust: in those days of despair, I experienced an odd pleasure from touching the dust, as if I was touching something similar to me, to my existence. It is now difficult for me to admit: other people's happiness hurt me at such times. I could not listen to the laughter reverberating through the street. Sometimes, if I heard sounds coming from that direction, I would move away from the corner in which I sat sheltered and would come closer to the window and squat underneath it; I would look through it furtively like a thief, like a criminal, like someone who was hiding; I would look with only a small part of my eye, with only a portion of my pupil. I saw people in the street, and I wondered if that was happiness and asked myself why I had never managed to be happy, although I believed that through my writings I would teach people how to live in happiness, peace, and freedom. However, not only had I failed to experience happiness, but during those days of despair, I did not even experience peace and freedom myself. I became imprisoned in my thoughts about things I could have done but had not done, and this created a frightening turmoil within me. Then I had to withdraw to one of the corners. I would put my fingers tightly in my ears and begin to hear a strange sound, akin to the distant howling of a wolf, that came from my chest.

Those days and nights always ended at the moment I was able to repeat to myself that despair was also an affection and that it could be overcome through understanding, but only if something allowed me to repeat it to myself. During those days and nights of despair, however much I tried to do that, some part of me would cut the thought halfway through. As soon as I started saying, "Despair is an affection arising from . . . ," the thought was abruptly cut as if by a blade, itself made of despair. And I really wanted to feel peaceful, grind lenses, write, play with the Spycks' children, walk in the streets, or go to the Old Tomcat tavern and have a glass of wine. I really wanted to be able to take my telescope and direct my gaze into the sky, into the stars.

During one such period of great despair, someone knocked at my door. I did not open it, I was sitting curled up in the corner, biting my knuckles. But soon there was another knock, after which I heard Mrs. Spyck's voice:

"Someone wants to see you."

They knew that whoever came to visit me on days like those had to be told not to disturb me, but the exception meant that someone special was looking for me. I got up, looked at my red eyes in the mirror, arranged my hair, and opened the door. Mrs. Spyck was not there anymore, only Clara Maria stood on the doorstep. When she saw me, she smiled in a strange way and let out an even stranger sound, as though she was trying to push a ball of sorrow away from the solar plexus to her throat.

"I've come to The Hague to see my auntie, and I wanted to see you too."

Astonishingly, I was no longer confused. I raised my hand and touched her left ear, made two movements around it and then touched her left and right nostrils, her mouth, and finally her forehead. Clara Maria started laughing, and in that laugh I recognized the same twelve-year-old girl I saw when I met her for the first time. She returned my greeting—she raised her hand, touched my left ear, made two movements around it, then touched my left and right nostrils, my mouth, and finally my forehead. The greeting immediately bridged the ten years that had elapsed since we last saw each other.

"Please, do sit down," I said, showing her to the chair near the table. She had changed a lot: her hair had lost its former glow; her walk, the way in which she limped used to be filled with joy; now it was a limp that indicated a certain distress not caused by the body, not by physical problems, it was a limp showing grief, as though she carried a bag full of hesitation, unfulfilled expectations, and sorrow. Her smell, however, had remained the same. We were sitting close to each other at the table, while she filled the silence by trying to move the strands of hair that fell over her face, with a puzzled smile, with the raising of her shoulders. I was inhaling the smell of her body, the smell that reminded me of whiteness, of whiteness so pure that even if drops of another color had fallen into it, it would have consumed them and stayed white.

"You know," she said, "I often remember . . . " She looked at the large red-canopied bed. "I often remember the first sentences of *The Anatomy of Melancholy* by Burton. . . ."

"*For those who are racked by melancholy, writing about it would have meaning only if writing sprang out of that very melancholy. I am trying to address an abyss of sorrow, a noncommunicable grief that at times, and often for a long time, lays claim upon us to the extent of having us lose all interest in words, action, and even life itself,*" I recalled, quoting her favorite passage from the book.

"Yes, that's right," she said and smiled. At that moment it appeared to me that she could not move her eyes away from the canopied bed, and I knew that whenever she remembered the passage from *The Anatomy of Melancholy,* she had to remember that night when the moon was full, when we were alone in her house, when she came to my room and sat close to me on the canopied bed, when I smelled of semen, and when she asked me why it was impossible to learn anything about the essence of things through smell, touch, taste, hearing, and sight.

"It's turned pale," she said, running her fingers over the canopied bed. "Are you comfortable here?" she asked, trying to get a wider view of the room, while her eyes returned to the bed again and again. "Yes, I am," I replied. I was looking at her legs, and then my eyes continued to slide between them. Guided by my obsession with innocence and at the same time by my awareness that it was no longer to be found there, in her crotch, I sought to establish the difference between innocence and its absence. "Are you writing something?" she asked, and I answered affirmatively, unaware of having said anything at all. I was only aware of my eyes constantly sliding from her pupils to her crotch, just as her eyes were repeatedly gliding from my face to the bed. "What are you writing?" she asked me, and again looked at the bed. I remembered the way she used to watch people. She watched them as though scrutinizing ten spots and would then choose the most interesting of all. Full of curiosity, she used to move her eyes rapidly from someone's eyes to their eyebrows, to their right ear and lower lip, and then to the middle of their forehead. Now I noticed that her look had acquired a certain weight while it formed a strange triangle, moving between my pupils, my hands, and the bed. "I'm writing about absence," I replied, unaware of what I had said, and she again drew the triangle between my pupils, my hands, and the bed. "About absence?" she asked. "No, I'm not writing about that at all," I answered. As her look stopped at my pupils, she saw my look descending yet again from her eyes to the place where her legs joined.

Then she showed me once again, just like she had shown me when she was a young girl, that it was not necessary to use the methods determined by reason in order to attain the third type of knowledge.

"Theodor can't do it," she said.

I remained silent.

"He can't do it," she repeated. She covered her knees with her hands. "I want a child," she said.

I did not say a word. If just a few moments ago I struggled to take my eyes away from her crotch, now they themselves ran away from her pupils. I was looking at her forehead and hair, I was looking at her hands on her lap, I was looking at her taut fingers, dug into her knees.

"I want a child," she repeated. The strange expectation in the air was hurting me. Her voice, both imploring and full of hope, seemed to be piercing my solar plexus, and the reflection of that sound was agonizing. The cry of one of the Spycks' children coming from one of the lower rooms seemed to relax the situation for a moment, but I saw that Clara Maria's face had suddenly become numb.

"I have to go now," she said and got up from her chair.

I wanted to say something, but I did not know what exactly. I followed her as we went down the stairs in silence.

"Will you come again?" I asked her, opening the door.

I do not remember what her answer was. In fact, I did not hear her answer at all, probably because the imploring tone and hope in her phrase still resonated in my ears. I was gazing into her face and I noticed a certain shiver there, a broken hope, and a reproach, hesitant as to where to go, toward me or back to herself. She smiled, to prevent her lips from twisting downward rather than wishing to express any warmth. She whispered that we would certainly see each other and that I was welcome to visit her and Theodor in Amsterdam. Then she just turned and walked away between the two rows of houses. I remained there, watching her disappear down the street: she walked slowly with the limp I knew so well. Her walk would remain in my memory as the most beautiful movement I had ever known in my life. I was sure that she could feel my eyes watching her. I even thought that she stopped for a moment, slightly turning her head, as if she wanted to turn around and see me once again, but, no, she walked on, speeding up a little. Those steps were the last thing I heard of her.

Yellow Flower

You will never see her again. She will often think of you, always when she hears the words *eternal* and *eternity*. When she thinks of you, of your choice to make her absent from your life, she will find an excuse for you in the absence of eternity in her life.

At times when her sorrow needs the company of sound, while she runs her fingers over the harpsichord keys (with its engraving "Music is the companion of joy and the remedy for suffering"; paradoxically, music will then only underscore her suffering), with each note she plays, she will always think of how brief the eternity of sound is.

And there is something you do not know, Spinoza. (But how could you have known it, you whom she has always asked, "What are you writing now?" while you have never asked her, "Do you write anything, Clara Maria?" You have not even asked yourself, "Does she, the most well-read person I know, write anything?") As she tries to fall asleep late at night, counting the hours by the church bell, sentences will flow, characters will be born, events will take place, novels will be born in her, but they will all die before they have opened their eyes and before their umbilical cord has been cut. She will never light the candle and write down the words that fill the hours before she falls asleep: not for fear of awakening Theodor, but because your obsession with eternity will become her obsession too. She will bury her unwritten works with the words, "Words do not fall into the void, but they never fall into eternity either. Words are transient."

When, one evening, having heard the news from one of his patients, Theodor tells her that you have died, she will shrug it off with a movement of her head, saying, "It isn't possible, he's not dead. He is eternal." If her husband hadn't believed that Clara Maria was joking, he would probably have thought she was crazy. But she is not joking, and she is not crazy: she truly believes in your eternity, Spinoza.

Shortly after your death, she will adopt a son, but death will serve to convince her of the transience and finiteness of things that can be seen, heard, smelled, tasted, or touched: Eeuwig (meaning "eternal" in Dutch) died when he was only nine.

Clara Maria will then travel alone all over Italy. The choice of this country is not accidental—she has chosen the company or aristocrats only because she can see in their palaces some of the recently discovered statues from classical antiquity, indicating that some things are nonetheless eternal. Her eyes, however, will be focused on details signifying transience: the statue of Venus lacks her left breast and fingers on her hands, Apollo is left without his phallus and right ear, and Cupid has lost his arrow. Clara Maria will be constantly wondering how long it will take until everything turns to dust.

While she walks in the squares and streets of Florence and Milan, homeless children will pull her by the sleeve, recognizing by the weary look in her eyes that this is a person ready to empty her pockets and fill their begging hands.

At one point she will even ask herself whether she has only per-haps accepted your idea of eternity as a defense against the anger she might feel toward you, lest she hate you for not fulfilling her expecta-tions. "Isn't it only a question of fear? If I didn't accept his fixation on eternal things, I might hate him for not sharing transient things with me," she will say to herself one morning in Venice, thinking about the reflection of her aged face in one of its canals.

She will die one morning in 1709 in Rome, the Eternal City, with a freshly picked yellow flower fading in her hand.

Dream

That night I had my first dream after Mother died. I could see myself in the dream. My eyes had an empty look. A bird was flying around me. I stretched my arm out and the bird landed on my hand. It was slowly dying, squirming in my hand. Then it suddenly rotted and worms began eating its flesh. I wanted to shake it off my hand, throw it on the ground, but I could not. It seemed to be stuck on me. I set off toward the house, toward our house, toward the house with the orange paint peeling off. Many people met me along the road, offer-ing me birds.

"Take them," they said. "They are for you."

I did not look at them. I was running toward the house; the dead bird in my hand was hurting me. I went through the door, but in-stead of going into the room, I suddenly found myself on the roof.

I looked down. In front of the house, between the main door and the canal, Mother lay on the large red-canopied bed.

"You've really grown old," she told me. "Now you look even older than me."

"I'll jump," I shouted.

"Don't," she said. "If you jump, you'll stay alive. Don't move!" and she turned around, toward the canal. She would not look at me anymore.

I did not jump. I woke up. I remained for a long time with my head buried in my hands. My hands sometimes smelled of carob and sometimes of a dead bird.

I felt I needed someone at that moment, someone to talk to. No, I did not want to talk about substance and essence, nor would I talk about attributes or modes. I wanted to talk about the simplest things. I imagined Clara Maria standing near the window. I could have asked her what she thought about the nature of affections or about the similarities and differences between the second and third types of knowledge. But there was no need to talk about such things. Not that I could not utter them with my mouth; they simply did not come to my mind.

"How much is a pound of fish?" I asked.

"I don't know," she answered. "I don't eat fish. I can't eat anything that has eyes," she said. "Theodor sometimes tells me, 'If you can't eat anything that has eyes, then why don't you eat moles?'"

"How is Theodor?"

"He has corns on his feet. He works a lot. Patients are always seeking him out."

"What about you?"

"I have no corns," she said, looking at her feet. She was barefoot.

"How are you?"

"I don't know. I no longer smell of the freshest milk; it's been a long time now." She looked at her fingers. "Now I think I know the meaning of those words from *The Anatomy of Melancholy: 'The departure of the indispensable person continues to deprive me of the most valuable part of myself. I see it as a wound or dispossession, only to discover that my pain is just a postponement of my hatred or of my desire to possess, which I am reserving for someone or something that has betrayed me or abandoned me.'*" She looked at me and smiled. "I dreamed of you," she said. "You sat in the corner with your mother, and you talked to each other. 'Am I disturbing you?' I asked. 'No,' your mother said, 'we're not eternal anyway.' But you said nothing. . . . You still have nothing to say."

"I know. I should say something, but I don't know what I'm supposed to say," and then I said nothing. She disappeared.

I needed someone to talk to, that is how I explained the appearance of Clara Maria in my thoughts, although I was scared by the fact that I saw her so clearly with my eyes open.

Johannes also appeared in my room once in a while. He was silent most of the time, and I did not dare ask him anything, though I wanted to know a lot of things about him. Once he told me:

"There are moments when all clothing is annoying to the body just as our thoughts are sometimes annoying to our mind."

THREAD SIX

He took his clothes off slowly, watching the excitement on my face. He approached me, took my hand and put it between his legs.

"Do you think infinity is harder than my penis?"

Just as I tried to compare infinity to his penis, Johannes vanished.

One evening, while I was sitting in the corner, Mother came to me and sat beside me.

"This is very strange," I told her.

"What is so strange?" she asked me.

"Me imagining you here," I said. "I wouldn't like you to think I was crazy, that I was talking to you while you're not here," I said.

"Don't worry," she said. "I'd never think that. What Mother would ever have thought that of her child, even if he was really crazy!"

"It's strange I can see you so clearly," I said.

"Why is it so strange?" she asked.

"I couldn't remember your face after you died."

"You didn't want to remember it," she said.

"You're right. I didn't want to remember it," I said. "Are you angry?"

"No," she said. "Why should I be angry?" I did not say anything. "Was it hard for you when I died?" she asked. "You were just a little boy then, a six-year-old."

"I don't remember," I said. "Even then I didn't want to remember it. I wanted to forget you were dead." She said nothing. "Grandfather came from Rotterdam. He must have grieved for you, but he never cried in front of us children. His eyes were red, though. But he never mentioned you. He gave me something, I can't remember what exactly—something to eat, or something to wear. I couldn't take it in my hand. I stretched out my arm but I couldn't open my fingers. I believed that everything I got as a present would disappear—I knew it would disappear. As though it had never existed. That's why I didn't want to possess anything right from the beginning. So that it wouldn't hurt me once I lost it. That's why I wanted to discover eternal things. That's why I decided to fall in love with God and not with a human being. Dead bodies, however, attracted me. Corpses, nothing else. I masturbated thinking of them. During the day, I would go to the Anatomy Theater, watching them being dissected, and I thought of them during the night. Living bodies never attracted me. Until one day when . . . "

Something rustled at the other end of the room. Close to the window, there stood Clara Maria.

"Am I disturbing you?" she asked.

"No," answered Mother. "We're not eternal anyway."

"Are you infinite?" asked Johannes, entering the room and closing the door behind him.

"By no means," answered Mother. "Look. Look how pale we are turning."

And indeed, their color was fading away, they were becoming thinner and thinner, turning into air.

I sighed, throwing my head back, hitting the wall, asking myself if I was going crazy: "Am I crazy? Am I crazy?"

"Is my mind sick too?" I was asking myself, feeling the sickness in my body. I could hardly breathe, I felt a crushing pain in my chest, I choked, and then pierced my vein with a needle to bleed myself, as my doctor had advised me.

Net

To save yourself from madness, you will draw. Later, years after your death, when Colerus comes to Hendrik van der Spyck's house to ask him to describe your life since he plans to write a book about you, your landlord will take your drawings from a drawer, and Colerus will write: "He taught himself the art of drawing, and he could sketch someone with ink or charcoal. I have in my hands a whole book of these, his art, in which he portrayed various considerable persons who were known to him and who visited him on occasion. Among other drawings, I found on the fourth sheet a fisherman in a shirt, sketched with a net on his right shoulder." Colerus may have examined the drawing carefully, but he failed to notice that the person in the drawing was not a fisherman, but you, and that it was not a fishing net on his shoulder, but a cobweb.

■ □ ■ □ ■

The cobweb has been dearer to me than any other form that expresses the bewilderment of all fragile things in the universe. Indeed, the cobweb has something in common with the labyrinth and the tree of life, though the differences outweigh the similarities.

The labyrinth was made by a man who wished to be God; the tree of life was made by people who wished to know the path of God's creation; the cobweb is made by God. No, please do not laugh, _____, the cobweb is indeed a creation of God. Who makes the thread that comes out of the spider's body? Who brings the wind? Who urges and helps the spider to spin thread after thread and tie them all together? Who can it be if not God—the eternal and infinite substance—that has taught the spider to build its cobweb?

The tree of life involves a hierarchy: it is divided into an upper and a lower part. The upper *sefirot* are closer to heaven, and the lower ones are closer to earth. There is also another apparently interesting classification, into male, female, and androgynous pillars, but what does it mean? Does victory, a characteristic of the seventh *sefira,* belong only to the male principle? Does glory, a characteristic of the eighth *sefira,* belong only to the female principle? And is beauty exclusively androgynous, bisexual? There is a hierarchy in the labyrinth as well: there are no upper and lower sections, as there are in the tree of life, and its hierarchy is not defined in terms of closeness to heaven or earth. Its hierarchy is established through the play of life and death: if you follow the right path that leads to the labyrinth's exit, you can continue your existence; if you choose the wrong path, you will find your death. And in the spider's creation—even though it has a center, it is not the most important spot—each spot is the center of the cobweb.

And finally, a few words about ingress and egress. The labyrinth has one or more entrances, but there is always but one exit. In the tree of life, you know exactly which *sefira* you can leave and enter through, and the paths you must follow: there are only three routes you can follow from Keter: toward Hokhma, Bina, and Tiferet. But in the cobweb you can leave from any point and arrive at any other point—every point is an entrance and an exit at the same time.

That was the reason I drew cobwebs, depicting them hanging over my shoulder, veiling my face, spread across the sky.

During the early November evenings that year, like any other year after Mother had died, I began breathing more heavily and rapidly, like you do when something is taken away from you, like you do when something is lost irretrievably. Sometimes, as I strained to take enough air into my lungs, Johannes would come and lie on the bed beside me.

"Write me a letter," he said.

"I don't know your address," I replied.

"The address doesn't matter. You just write me a letter," he said and disappeared.

I would get up, sit at the table, and begin writing. I wrote the letter with one hand and tore it up with the other.

"Now you know," I sometimes heard Clara Maria's voice in the night, "now you know why, when we played the quotations game, I always ended the game with Ovid's lines about Narcissus."

"I know," I said.

"And you also know why I cried that night before you left our house, when I recited the passage about Echo the nymph to you."

"Yes, I know now," I said. "But I didn't know it then. Had I known it, I would not perhaps have fallen in love with a shadow, as Narcissus did. He, in the reflection of his body; I, in the reflection of my mind. Both he and I fell in love with reflections, mere shadows."

"It seems that it is only my voice and my bones that are left of me now, just as happened to Echo."

"I can only hear your voice," I said to her.

"Soon you won't be able to hear even that," she said, and then there was silence.

I was sitting alone in my room. It was a sultry February night, and my heavy breathing was reminding me of Mother's death.

21 February 1677

Today is 21 February, Spinoza, the same day as your conception that night almost forty-five years ago in Amsterdam. Today is 21 February, night is falling, and this is the night when you will die. Can you feel it when you begin to cough, taking a sip of milk whose taste you can no longer discern? You put the glass back on the table, but you do not feel that you are holding it in your hand; it is the same as if you were touching an empty space. You get up and go to the window. You open it. "It should smell of winter outside," you are thinking, but only some kind of bitter smell reaches your nostrils. Your vision is blurred: you can see everything—the street, the snow, the church roof—and yet everything in front of you is empty. Sounds come to you, but they do not reach you: you can hear them, but you no longer know what you are hearing. Are you anxious, Spinoza?

I know, a free man thinks least of all of death, but perhaps there is something that urges you to turn around, to look at the things that have remained behind, or perhaps, things that could have remained behind, but you have done nothing to see to that. Do you feel sad about having not done certain things, Spinoza? You leave the window open and you approach the canopied bed.

You are dying, Spinoza, and I have to leave you here alone with your death, as the encounter with death is always faced alone.

■ □ ■ □ ■

THE CENTER OF THE COBWEB

Death

I have a presentiment that I am about to die. *I repeated this to myself,
although somewhere deep within myself I hoped that a mistake was a
possibility in any presentiment; I repeated this to myself that evening
when death was inexorably drawing nearer and nearer.* Yes, I will die
tonight, *I told myself over and over again, probably wishing to drive
fear of death away by becoming aware of the coming of the end, to scare
fear away.*

I feel an ever increasing pain in my chest, and the pain makes me
close my eyes; this pain or the awareness that I cannot see what I am
supposed to see with my own eyes, *or perhaps the fear of death made
me stare into the darkness of my closed eyes* and memories of the day of
my excommunication arise from this darkness; it was the same then,
I also felt pain in my chest, but it was a different kind of pain. Then
I felt the pain of alienating myself from those with similar blood to
mine; now I feel the pain of alienating myself from my own blood;
then, too, I thought I was losing the ground from under my feet, but
I boldly stepped into the new day, and now I am falling to the floor;
*then, at the moment when I was dying, it seemed to me that I was falling
into nothingness, where there was neither eternity nor infinity, and I felt
so lost, so broken; it seemed to me that if I only opened my eyes, I would
see the separation of my soul from my body, yearning to preserve my body,
to preserve myself in that body, although it was totally useless, its senses
already dead, and feeling that fear, I kept my eyes closed while I was falling to the floor, toward nothingness, into the finite and limited.*

I have fallen on the floor and I am trying to stand up; I manage to stand up and sit on the red-canopied bed, *which was perhaps no longer red; time had changed its color as well, just as it had changed the color of my skin;* I begin to cough, the pain is more and more intense. I lie down on the canopied bed and I curl up like a fetus, *and my thoughts were cutting through the waters of remembrance, cutting, like a ship, through those waters that used to create whirlpools and did not let me get closer to every moment of my past, and that ship sailed on and on, hastening forward, or rather, backward, before I fled from life into philosophy, before getting rid of Johannes because of my fear of corporeality, before I fled with my definitions from Clara Maria's sensuality, before my excommunication, before the death of Mother; that ship sailed faster and faster, combining the stone pieces of my past into a single mosaic composition, irresistibly reminiscent of my being, of my true I, of that I for which I had searched all my life and which was being revealed to me at that fateful moment.*

I am lying on the bed curled up like a fetus; *life lay on my left-hand side, and death on my right;* I am lying there and crawling deeper and deeper inside myself, looking for the place where eternity and infinity are born, the place that has not, not even for an instant, shown itself to me in life, although I have been searching for it all the time while writing, or even more so while thinking about what to write, while thinking about existence; now I am sinking into my own soul, now I am sinking into my own *I,* and I realize that the soul gives birth to both the eternal and the infinite, that the soul exists only to express eternity and infinity, and at the same time I understand that such an attempt is infinitely futile, since eternity and infinity are not enough to explain the soul, and the soul is too small to encompass eternity and infinity. *At that moment a burning pain hit my body and my soul, a pain that came from the realization of the impossibility of explaining the soul through eternity and infinity, or encompassing eternity and infinity through the soul. This could nonetheless be a possibility through the body, that the soul examined eternity and infinity through the body; curled up like a fetus, I then looked at certain parts of my body, I saw my thickened nails, my contorted fingers, and then the burning pain became more and more intense; I thought this was the end, I thought I was parting with my body, I thought this was the moment when I parted with both my body and the possibility of touching eternity and infinity, by walking along their edge through my senses. I felt no sadness, not even sadness could exist anymore, everything had come to an end, I only thought that everything around me was disappearing, everything that I used to want to disappear so that I could experience myself in my separateness. At that instant, however, I wished, if I could manage to wish anything anymore, to be given a new chance to exist, like a writer who, having written a bad book, wishes to be given a chance to write it again.*

I am lying on the bed, I am lying there curled up like a fetus, *and I felt as if my soul were moving up and down, as if it were trying to penetrate the membrane of my body, and at the same time, wanted to strengthen that membrane, to slow down its inevitable disintegration; I was lying there curled up like a fetus and I realized that the moment was drawing near when the straight line of my life would swerve and turn into a circle, where the beginning and the end would touch each other and be lost in one another; I was lying there curled up like a fetus while my mind went back to my earliest memories, and then went back even further, to the first moments of my existence; my thoughts moved between the legs of my mother, they crawled back into her womb,* and I can now see myself sailing in the waters of my mother's womb, curled up and with my eyes closed like now, devoid of questions like now; *yes, then, for the first time after becoming separated from my mother's womb I had no questions, since, by collecting all the images from my past into a single synchronicity, all my questions were answered immediately, without a word, and all that I wanted was to go back to my mother's womb, to be born once again, but with all the knowledge I had gathered while I was falling, while I lay on the canopied bed curled up like a fetus; I believed in the endless joy of existence of that being that knew the true breadth, depth, and weight of one's own* I, *of that* I *that hid itself from me at the times when I searched for it most persistently and when it seemed I was just about to find it; this* I *was hiding itself from me behind my own shadow, behind my own voice, behind the farthest point on the horizon;* and now, at last, I can see that *I* of mine, now while I am lying on this canopied bed, attuned to my own blood cooling down.

Birth

It is nighttime, Spinoza, and I am turning the last pages of this novel. Tonight is as dense as the night of the twenty-fourth day of November, the date of your birth, the night when Rembrandt is completing his *Anatomy Lesson of Professor Nicolaes Tulp*. It is nighttime,

Spinoza, and I feel tired in a particular way, perhaps in the same way as Rembrandt will feel after completing his painting. The book slowly drops from my hands, and Rembrandt lets his brush drop as well. Rembrandt drops his brush at the precise moment he completes the section he wanted to start from, but that he left until the end, that drop of blood between the fingers of Professor Nicolaes Tulp— the last proof that the dead man was once alive. It is you, however, who has the most life at this precise moment. It is you who was the most alive that night just as you are tonight, Spinoza. It is precisely at this instant that you are being born, both that night and tonight. Your mother is lying on the bed with her legs spread out, and your little head emerges from her womb. Her scream is strong enough to reach the house in which Rembrandt steps back, looks at his canvas, and then approaches it again. No, he is not particularly interested in *The Anatomy Lesson* as a whole. His pupils are concentrated on that drop of blood, on that piece of the human soul between Professor Tulp's fingers. While they are taking you out of your mother's womb, dear Spinoza, I myself appear from somewhere, running with a forceps in my hand, that same forceps Professor Nicolaes Tulp holds in Rembrandt's painting. I am to stay for just a brief moment, only to cut your umbilical cord, and then to disappear yet again beyond the pages of this book, wishing you a happy life.

INSTEAD OF AN EPILOGUE:
WHY SPINOZA?

Why, indeed, Spinoza?

All writers, as well as constantly striving to answer the question why they write at all, often ask themselves why they have chosen to write about a particular subject. Yes, why, indeed, Spinoza? The following pages are an attempt to offer an answer to these questions, an attempt to find a likely explanation.

I knew that I would write about Spinoza the first time I heard of him—in grammar school, at a philosophy class given by my teacher, Gordana Gurčinovska. Had I written about him then, the answer would have been more or less obvious: I would have chosen him because of his (and not only his) loneliness. Yes, it was not his philosophy that attracted me then; it was his life that appealed to me: the outcast sage whom Jews were not allowed to approach and who earned his living by grinding lenses. That is how I felt then, and after a while, it seemed I had forgotten Spinoza completely: I was too busy writing about other things. When the idea of writing about him came back to me two years ago, I started with my philosophy notebook from my grammar school days and a heap of books. At first I read all of his work and then all the biographies—written by his contemporaries Jean-Maximilian Lucas and Johan Colerus, as well as our own contemporaries Margaret Gullan-Whur and Steven Nadler. The explanations of his teaching were the last on my list.

Gilles Deleuze, the great, and probably the greatest, interpreter of Spinoza's philosophy, wrote the following in a letter to the English translator of his book, *Expressionism in Philosophy:* "What interested me most in Spinoza wasn't his Substance, but the composition of finite modes" (M. Joughlin, translator's preface, in Gilles Deleuze, *Expressionism in Philosophy,* Zone Books, New York, 1990).

Yes, this is something that can definitely arouse the interest not only of a philosopher but also a novelist—not substance, not eternal things, but limited, finite modes, or to put it simply: ourselves and everything around us. The difference is that the philosopher (Deleuze, in this case), owing to the different natures of philosophy and literature, is interested in Spinoza's finite modes for the purpose of "seeing in substance *a plane of immanence* in which finite modes operate," and the novelist is more interested in the philosopher Spinoza's interpretation of finite modes, because Spinoza as a human being is expressed through that interpretation. And Spinoza as a human being, judging from what Spinoza as a philosopher said, averted his eyes from everything that was finite and transient. Judging from Spinoza's writings, we can assume that he was a passionless man led by reason along a smooth (and rather tedious) path of existence. But everything is not so smooth in the pages of his works. This is what Deleuze has written in another of his books in which he reexamines the teachings of Bento/Baruch/Benedictus:

"The *Ethics* is a book written twice simultaneously: once in the continuous stream of definitions, propositions, demonstrations, and corollaries, which develop the great speculative themes with all the rigors of the mind; another time in the broken chain of scholia, a discontinuous volcanic line, a second version underneath the first, expressing all the angers of the heart and setting forth the practical theses of denunciation and liberation" (Gilles Deleuze, *Spinoza: Practical Philosophy,* trans. Robert Hurley, San Francisco, City Lights, 1988, 28–29).

Deleuze believes that Spinoza's *Ethics* was written twice and that its duality can be followed in parallel. But if it were indeed written twice and if reason was predominant in some parts, whereas other parts are characterized by "a discontinuous volcanic line" that expresses "all the angers of the heart," it must have been written by a man who was deeply divided inside himself, in whom reason and passion fought a constant battle, a man who lived in despair precisely because of the split. True, I have no proof of Spinoza's despair other than his portrait dating from a few years before his death. But can there be a better witness to a man's life than the expression on his face, the expression of a man who constantly warned of despair as a negative "affection" and yet was unable to hide it when he was being portrayed?

It is because of this split in Spinoza's soul that I decided to divide the novel into two main sections. This involved a different, parallel approach to all the definitions and propositions from his *Ethics:* what was put forward in the first section was shattered in the second. The novel's first section deals with a Spinoza who thinks, a typical *homo intellectualis,* who turns, in the second section, into a *homo sentimentalis.* In the first section, he thinks; in the second, he feels. This approach has resulted in a certain parallelism between Spinoza as a character and the character of the reader: what the reader could only vaguely sense in the novel's first section Spinoza imparts in the second section.

The characters of Clara Maria van den Enden and Johannes Casearius are also parallel. The association of Clara Maria with eternity/transience and of Johannes with infinity/finiteness was established depending on the places in which the lives of these characters (also real people) ended. Clara Maria died in Rome, the Eternal City, and Johannes (whose book on botany was published posthumously) died of dysentery in Malabar, India, the land that took so long to get to that it seemed like the end of the world, on the doorstep of infinity.

As far as parallelism is concerned, Deleuze also finds it in Spinoza's philosophy, dividing it into the epistemological and ontological. Epistemological parallelism, according to Deleuze, is established between the idea and its object, whereas ontological parallelism occurs between all the modes that are differentiated in an attribute.

■ □ ■ □ ■

I believe that every author's intention is to write for the sake of beauty as well. Every writer wishes to write a beautiful book. The motives may be different, but the goal is always the same. On the other hand, Spinoza has always been criticized for his philosophy being overly concentrated on ethics and totally neglecting aesthetics. His philosophy lacks beauty; it is sterile and tiresome, say the scholars. This is probably so. The objective of his philosophy, however, is beauty nonetheless—the beauty of existence. Hoping to teach people not only to think properly but also to live properly (that is, happily, peacefully, and fully), I am certain that Spinoza believed that he could turn their lives into a thing of beauty equaling infinity and eternity. Partly because of this aim, it is beauty that was actually lacking from his everyday life: excommunication, no permanent residence, poverty, solitude. So when I was writing this *Conversation with Spinoza*, I knew exactly why I wanted to write a beautiful book. I wanted to give beauty to Spinoza's solitude. That is why I could not end my novel in any other way than by wishing him a happy life: the novel ends by giving the opportunity to the great philosopher to live a part of life on earth again. This aim—to give beauty to someone's solitude—while it may add beauty to the book from the viewpoint of ordinary human beings, can rob it of some of its beauty according to the criteria of the critics. This novel has no irony, distance, or cynicism, the three key principles preached by the interpreters of postmodernism, to which this work certainly does not belong. This may be the most belated work of romanticism—universally scorned in this "age of intelligence." Sentimentality is deliberately set out here as the opposite of rationality.

■ □ ■ □ ■

In the beginning I was afraid that I would be unable to understand the philosophy of Spinoza. Now I know that I probably did not understand it completely. And this is not that bad. But in the beginning I was afraid that I might wrongly interpret the basic postulates of Spinoza's philosophy with the consequence that the novel that was aimed at the moon might shoot at the sun. My fear persisted until I read Pierre Macherey's text "The Encounter with Spinoza." The author of this paper claims (and also demonstrates) with great assurance that Deleuze, the greatest authority on Spinoza, made several major errors in his interpretation of the Dutch philosopher's work. I took *Expressionism in Philosophy: Spinoza* and *Spinoza: Practical Philosophy* from my shelf. I read them once again and I finally felt enlightened: Deleuze's goal was not to reach absolute truth (which undoubtedly does not exist); his goal was playfulness. Deleuze knows how to play with words, definitions, and propositions. He does not even try to be fully faithful to Spinoza's philosophy when he interprets him. What is important to Deleuze is to show that he has experienced him—even if, and above all, by means of reason, as becomes a real philosopher.

It was then that I felt myself free to play. The novel upsets the chronology of the development of some of Spinoza's concepts: when he speaks about them to Clara Maria and Johannes, these concepts were still in their inception phase. But, as I said, my goal was playfulness, my objective was to tell a story. If there are indeed errors in the interpretation of Spinoza in the novel, a justification can easily be found: his views at the time were still not fully developed, so perhaps he did understand substance and modes, affections and knowledge in precisely that way. I allowed myself the greatest freedom when I explained substance, attributes, essence, eternal and infinite modes, as well as transient and finite modes to Clara Maria as light, body of light, prisms, play of light. . . . This is one of the tasks of any author—to be free and to play when he writes, communicating things from his own point of view. In fact, Gilles Deleuze describes attributes in exactly the same way: different attributes are actually different points of view of the same thing. All of us see the same thing—the movement of living creatures through time and space—each of us being an attribute for himself or herself (or rather, an observer, and sometimes a storyteller as well), with his or her own point of view.

In any case, Deleuze's interpretations were of great help to me, so much so that while I was writing the novel, I sometimes had the feeling it was being written by three hands simultaneously: two right hands (Spinoza's and mine) and one left hand (Deleuze was purportedly left-handed).

■ □ ■ □ ■

In a book, I came across the title of another quoted work, *The Anatomy of Melancholy* by Robert Burton, published in London in 1621. I immediately wanted to include this work in my *Conversation with Spinoza*. I thought it was a great idea to cite several sentences from a work that was not only an anatomy of melancholy but also was an anatomy of melancholy in another work in which a melancholic child grew in his mother's womb, while in the course of the same nine months another melancholic person painted *The Anatomy Lesson of Professor Nicolaes Tulp*. As this was a time when I was working on my master's thesis at the Central European University, I thought that a copy of the book could be found in or via Budapest, a reprint or a microfilm copy. Then I had another idea—one of the concepts I dealt with in my thesis was melancholia as interpreted by Julia Kristeva in her work *Black Sun* (*Soleil Noir*). I thought it could be exciting to quote a contemporary writer, while referring to the title and author of a work written nearly four centuries ago. So wherever there are "quotations" from *The Anatomy of Melancholy* by Robert Burton, these are in fact borrowed passages from Julia Kristeva's *Black Sun: Depression and Melancholia*. Some of the concepts in Kristeva's book, as well as those in books by Shoshana Felman, Richard Rorty, Jasmina Lukic, Mikhail Bakhtin, Elizabeth Grosz, Judith Butler, Patricia Waugh, Mieke Bal, Shlomith Rimmon-Kenan, and Susan S. Lanser, were signs to me as I walked in the labyrinth of the conversation with Spinoza.

■ □ ■ □ ■

The reason for Spinoza's excommunication from the Jewish community remains unknown and, as one of his biographers says, "will probably remain always hidden to us." I had no idea what to cite as the reason for the rabbis' curse on Baruch. The reason is not mentioned in the proclamation (*cherem*) by the elders. The text of the excommunication itself does not point to anything specific, neither is there any reference to this in Spinoza's letters or in any other document from that time. I was thinking of all the possible inanities due to which a man could be excommunicated. I finally had the idea that the easiest way to embitter the priests is to preach knowledge that would only be accepted in the future, but certainly not at that time. So I decided to introduce the character of Accipiter Beagle, from whom Spinoza had received the forbidden knowledge. The postulates are, of course, taken from the theory of evolution by Charles Darwin and from Stephen Hawking's *A Brief History of Time*. I chose the name Accipiter Beagle for the character who propagated Darwin's theory. Accipiter means "hawk" in Latin, and Beagle—apart from sounding similar to Mount Bigla in Macedonia, where Accipiter was born—is identical to the name of the ship on which Darwin sailed during his scientific expedition.

■ □ ■ □ ■

In view of the teachings of the man whose entire life was dedicated to ethics (his major work is entitled *Ethics*), readers could ask the question whether it is indeed ethical to write about events in Spinoza's life that may never have happened. Is it ethical to write about someone's passion, despair, or hopes, even if these may never have occurred? What comes to my mind first is Miguel de Unamuno's maxim that "Don Quixote is no less true than Cervantes, and Hamlet and Macbeth are no less true than Shakespeare." In this sense, the Spinoza who lives in this novel is no less true than the Spinoza who lived from 1632 to 1677, just as the reader in the book is no less true than the reader who actually holds this book in his or her hands. As a matter of fact, just as geometry teaches us that two parallel lines cross each other in infinity, I believe that all of us will meet one another at a certain point. Perhaps in infinity. The Spinoza from this novel will meet the Spinoza of real flesh and blood, and the reader in this novel will meet the reader of this novel, while at the same time all the lines in that absolute parallelism will meet at a single point. Absolute identity will be achieved between the two Baruchs, the readers, and the author. Obviously, everything is possible in infinity. And everything is one.

■ □ ■ □ ■

Once again, why Spinoza?

When I was talking to Dime T. from Ohrid, Macedonia, one afternoon about parapsychology, he asked me: "Why do you think you are writing about Spinoza?" Had it been a conversation with a philosopher, I would have said something like: "Because of his unique philosophy, because of his divergence from Descartes' doctrine about God's free will and the body-soul dichotomy." Had I talked to a literary theoretician, I would have answered her: "I have long wanted to try a new narrative approach—to write a novel as a conversation taking place between the reader and a character." But I knew I was talking to someone who knew the truth even before I said anything. So I chose not to say anything (I later learned that he knew the truth even when I had forgotten it). I felt I had to answer his question honestly, but I did not know the answer. "You've been so lonely, Goce. Why?" Dime T. said, answering with a query, and carried me back to the time I seemed to have forgotten, where there still existed "the subdued sickness of pain" (Kristeva).

"A writer," says Vladimir Nabokov, "is born in solitude." He is not only born in solitude—he also exists in solitude. Writing itself is an act of solitude. Or perhaps a need to overcome solitude. A need for conversation. Hence these conversations. Hence this *Conversation with Spinoza*.

Hence Spinoza.

ABOUT THE AUTHOR

Goce Smilevski was born in Skopje in 1975 and studied comparative litera-ture at Sts. Kiril and Metodij University in Skopje and Czech literature at Universita Karlova in Prague. He earned a master's degree in gender studies from the Central European University in Budapest, where he wrote his the-sis on Milan Kundera. *Conversation with Spinoza* was written in 2002 and won the Macedonian national Novel of the Year Award.

■ □ ■ □ ■

WRITINGS FROM AN UNBOUND EUROPE

For a complete list of titles, see the Writings from an Unbound Europe Web site at
www.nupress.northwestern.edu/ue.